KIDNAPPED

KIDNAPPED

A Tugboater's Tale

BOB OJALA

A3Pi Services, LLC

Contents

ACKNOWLEDGEMENTS

In my previous novels, I explained how important an Editor can be to an author, and I know it may have sounded overly dramatic. I gave a lot of credit to my Editor, Nicole Amma Twum-Baah! (AmmaEdits.com)

This novel had a much more complicated story to tell, because of the subject matter, and I wanted everything to be properly told. The stories in my mind appeared on the written page, but may not have been as well organized as they should be. Amma again performed her magic, and the story began to flow properly with her help and was vastly improved.

Once again, Amma, I cannot thank you enough!

KIDNAPPED – A TUGBOATER'S TALE

Chapter 1

CURT

"Dad, we've got a bad problem. Tell me what to do."

My son, Steve, was crewing on our new tugboat acquisition. They were picking up a couple of barges near Chicago. It was summer, and Steve, a third-year Naval Architecture student at the University of Michigan was trying to round out his maritime resume by working as a tugboat deckhand with the company I work for. Normally, I try to have Steve on a tug where I am the captain, but occasionally, I send him along with a job where I cannot be aboard.

This summer, I had hired Steve as a crew member, relieving other tug deckhands who wanted some extra time off to spend with their families. That's the biggest drawback of this job, being away from home for weeks at a time during the good summer weather when their kids are out of school.

But now, I heard the tremble in Steve's voice, and I knew something was really wrong.

"What's wrong, Steve? I can hear it in your voice."

"Captain Ashley and Adam went ashore a few hours ago to buy some pizza for the crew. They called an Uber to take them out to pick up the pizzas, because the pizza place refused to deliver them down here, along the Indiana Harbor Canal. Adam told me they'd be back in thirty or forty minutes, but they never came back."

"How long have they been gone, son?"

"It's been almost three hours. I had their cell phone numbers, so I started calling them after it got over an hour, but they didn't answer. I even called the local Uber office to see where they had gone. I only remembered it started with a 'P', but Uber said they couldn't release that information. I'm pretty sure something bad must have happened. What should I do?"

"Where's the tug tied up, Steve?"

"We're in Indiana Harbor. We're docked at some old coal dock, waiting to pick up those barges tomorrow morning."

I didn't want to mention it to Steve, but Indiana Harbor is not a place for sailors to go ashore. The plan had been for the tug to stay in the Calumet River, in South Chicago, then go to Indiana Harbor to get the barges once they were loaded. That Indiana Harbor dock is nestled between two steel mills, an oil refinery, and a lot of dark streets full of questionable bars. Why had Ashley and Adam decided to take the tug into Indiana Harbor to spend the night, and then to order pizza in a place like that? And why on earth had they gone out at night to pick them up? If the pizza place refused to make a delivery, that should have been a big warning.

"Who else is on the tug with you, Steve?

"We have the new mate, the one they call Chubby, and three deckhands. Chubby and I are still up, waiting. Chubby's in the pilothouse on watch, and I sent the three deckhands down to bed an hour ago."

"I think it's time to call the police, Steve. Dial '9-1-1' and tell them you have two missing crew members in East Chicago. Then call me back. Once you've talked with the police, we can decide what to do next."

"Okay, Dad. I'm really scared. What do you think happened to them?"

"I'm worried too, Steve. That's not a place to be off the tug at night. Let's hope for the best. We'll talk again once you've talked to the '9-1-1' dispatcher. Just tell them where you are and that two people are missing."

"Okay, Dad. I'll call you back."

"Make that call right away, son."

After hanging up the call, I thought about Steve and the situation he was dealing with. I knew he was in a vulnerable position and had probably held off calling me because he didn't want to embarrass his captain, Ashley.

Ashley and her husband Adam were both missing, and I was worried about them. If they went to a place in Whiting to get the pizza, that's a relatively safe place, but getting there from that coal dock on the Indiana Harbor Canal means going through some very rough neighborhoods. Steve had mentioned that they called an Uber, but not all Uber drivers can be trusted, especially the ones who are local and could probably tell that Ashley and Adam were out of their element.

Captain Ashley was a tiny woman, not anything like you'd expect a tugboat captain to look like, but she could be tough when needed. About eight years ago, while I was training her, readying her to sit for her Coast Guard master's license exam, our tug was on a trip up on Lake Superior when we had a man overboard near the Keweenaw Peninsula. Well, it turned out to be a woman overboard, and Ashley was the one in the water. She remained so calm throughout the entire ordeal that she quickly gained the respect of her crewmen.

It was during that overboard incident that Ashley met her husband, Adam, and their relationship started. They got serious about one another shortly afterward and had since been married for about a year. The company did its best to keep them working together.

Adam Walters was currently the tug's licensed engineer, and as much as everyone loved him, he was sort of a simple, back-woods kinda' guy. Ashley, on the other hand, normally just worked the construction sites in the northern Lakes' ports. Both were wonderful people, but both were also very naïve about many things.

Chapter 2

STEVE

It didn't take long for the police to arrive at the tug. The East Chicago Police force was used to having sailors in town. Ships arrived frequently with iron ore and coke to the steel mills, and the tug/barge tankers brought petroleum products from the refinery. Typically, such calls were about sailors being drunk and disorderly at a local tavern, so hearing that two sailors were missing, was somewhat unusual.

An older policeman approached Steve, followed by a much younger officer. The older of the two was a handsome, Hispanic man, graying at the temples.

"I'm Sergeant Hernandez," he said to Steve. Then gesturing to the younger officer, he continued, "and this is Officer Simmons. I understand that you called because two of your crew members are missing?" Steve noticed that the man had no accent whatsoever.

Steve explained that the captain and chief engineer, who happened to be husband and wife, had ordered pizza, and called for an Uber to go and pick up the order. They had been expected to return 30 to 40 minutes later, and it had now been almost three hours.

"Hmmm," the sergeant murmured after scribbling something down in the small notepad in his hand.

Officer Simmons chuckled softly.

"I didn't get alarmed for an hour or so, and then I kept calling their cell phones," Steve quickly added, sensing that the officers did not see the emergency of the situation. "When they never answered, I decided to call my father. He's the Operations Manager for the tug owner. My dad then told me to call the police."

"Mr. Steiner," Sergeant Hernandez said, closing his notepad. "The people you describe here are adults. Don't you think it's possible they went somewhere else before heading back here? Perhaps, as husband and wife, they decided to go sightseeing, to visit a friend..."

"...Or, you know...get drunk, get some privacy..." Officer Simmons added while chuckling and winking at Sergeant Hernandez.

Sergeant Hernandez did not wink back or chuckle. Steve saw that as a hopeful sign.

"No, they would have said something to me. These are two responsible people who went out to pick up a couple pizzas for all of us and are now not answering their phones. Neither one of them is answering their phones! Captain Ashley would have called or sent the Uber driver back here with the pizzas if she knew they were going to be longer than she said they were going to be."

Sensing Steve's despair, the sergeant reopened his notepad and asked Steve, "Do you know which pizza place they called?"

"I don't remember, but I think I would recognize the name if I heard it. I think it started with a P."

"Paisano's?" Officer Simmons asked.

"Does that sound right?" Sergeant Hernandez asked Steve, who was now nodding his head.

"Yes, that's it," Steve said.

"So, is your father coming to the tug, since you've called him?"

"My dad is at home in Cadillac, Michigan. I'd hate for him to drive all this way if we can find the captain and Adam soon."

"Okay, Steve. If you feel confident in safeguarding the tug and helping us to find your crewmembers ---"

"--- Oh sure. I have a licensed mate aboard and three deckhands. We're fine, But I'm worried about Captain Ashley and Adam."

"So, give me the full names of these two, missing people, Steve."

"It's Ashley Walters and Adam Walters. They're married, I think I may have told you."

"Yes, you had mentioned that. Do you happen to know their address?"

"Not their full address, but I think they moved to Traverse City when they married."

"That's Traverse City, Michigan? Right?"

"Yes."

"Now, there are two Paisano's within close driving distance, so that may have been part of the confusion. They may just be lost. Do you know which one they called?"

"I don't know which one they called, but that would mean they've been lost nearly three hours, and as I told you, they're also not answering their phones."

"We'll also check that out, Steve. We'll ask their phone service provider to try to locate their phones. But you said they took an Uber from the tug?"

"Yes. I called the local Uber number, but they won't give out information on rides. But Sergeant Hernandez, we need to take this seriously. I probably need to call this in to the U.S. Coast Guard next, because these two crew members are licensed maritime officers, and the Coast Guard needs to be notified. I'm sure the Captain of the Port in Chicago will be calling to be sure your department is doing everything possible to locate these people."

"I'll pass that on to our Lieutenant," Hernandez said. "I have your card, and here's mine. I'll keep you informed."

Steve took the card from Sergeant Hernandez and watched the two officers leave the tug. He hoped they would prove helpful. He wasn't sure about Officer Simmons, but he hoped Sergeant Hernandez knew the seriousness of the situation.

East Chicago is a tough, steel mill town, and he

feared the police might overlook the incident as just a couple out having fun as Officer Simmons and Sergeant Hernandez had insinuated Steve, however, knew the kind of crew that worked for Strauss Marine, and a captain who had worked for them for several years was going to be a responsible individual and not go out looking for trouble.

Alone on the tug with four other guys not that much older than he was, Steve began to wish they had stayed in Chicago instead of coming to the Indiana Harbor Canal. It was safer over in the Calumet River.

The original plan was for the tug to come to Indiana Harbor in the morning to pick up the barges, but Steve had heard Captain Ashley talking with Adam that morning. She said because the barge loading had been delayed, she thought they'd save time by coming to Indiana Harbor that afternoon, and then they could leave as soon as the barges were loaded the next morning. But when they arrived, the dock manager told the captain that the barges wouldn't be ready until late tomorrow. The captain must have wanted to make the crew feel better by getting those pizzas, but now it had turned into a disaster.

Steve was no longer thinking positively. It wasn't something as simple as just getting lost. Two naïve people out in a dangerous neighborhood and not answering their phones did not add up to a happy ending. Steve was just hoping they would be found safe and unharmed.

Steve decided to call his dad again with an update,

and Curt was obviously upset. Strauss Marine treated their tug crews and construction workers like a big family, and they always bragged about the fact that everyone was watching their fellow crew members' backs. Now, Curt had a licensed captain and chief engineer missing, under possible dire circumstances, and Curt felt helpless to assist them.

"I just spoke with your Uncle Bill, son. As you can imagine, he's very upset and worried. Do you think I should head for Chicago?"

"And just what would you do here, Dad? You can worry about the situation from there, just like you would if you were here. The tug is secure, and the mate and deckhands are doing fine. If Ashley and Adam aren't found by morning, we can decide what happens next. The barges won't be ready to leave until late tomorrow. For now, you stay put. I can handle things here."

"You're sure you have things under control?" Curt asked.

"We're fine on the tug. I know how to change over the generators and start the main engines if I have to. The mate said he could move the tug if we needed to do it, and these deckhands are good guys."

Just then, Steve's phone rang, and it appeared to be Sergeant Hernandez. "I'd better get this call, dad. It looks like the East Chicago Police on the line."

"Okay. Call me back," Curt said.

"Steve Steiner," Steve said, taking the call.

"Sergeant Hernandez here. No word on your crew

members yet, but we were able to track down their Uber driver. It's a local guy, Trevor Jordan. I happen to know him personally. He's a decent family man, driving Uber in his free time. He works days at the refinery."

"Have you talked to him? Did he have any information on my crewmen?" Steve asked.

"I talked with his wife. She gave me his cell phone number, but I'm not getting an answer."

"What do we do next?" Steve asked.

"I've sent a car to Paisano's Pizza. It was hard to talk over the noise when I called over there. I'll let you know what we find out from them."

A few minutes later, Sergeant Hernandez called to say that the crewmen had, in fact, showed up at Paisanos. And because there were two locations in the area, captain Ashley and Adam directed the Uber driver to the wrong place. They had gone to the location on Calumet Avenue in Hammond. Rather than drive from there to the Whiting location, where they had placed their order, the Hammond store called the Whiting store, which was able to cancel the first order so they could remake them in Hammond.

"Your crewmen sat in Hammond while they made the new pizzas for them. The restaurant manager told us your guys released the Uber driver, even though he offered to wait with them. While they waited, the manager saw them strike up a conversation with a young couple eating in the restaurant, and those people offered to drive your guys back to the tug. The manager said he had seen that couple several times before and they were a nice couple, and they had expressed interest in seeing the tug. He didn't think they would have harmed your crew members. They left as soon as the two pizzas were ready."

"And that's now almost four hours ago," Steve said. "Does that mean we now have four missing people?"

"That's certainly what we're thinking. Luckily, the couple paid by credit card, so we were able to get the man's name from the manager. The watch commander is calling their credit card company right now, trying to get contact information for the fella who offered your people the ride. As soon as we contact that person, we'll call to update you again."

"Thanks, Sergeant. Would you also call me if you cannot locate that young man? As you might imagine, I'm more worried as time passes."

"No problem, Mr. Steiner. I'll call in 30 minutes unless we locate him sooner."

"Great. Thank you."

"Any updates on the missing crewmen situation?" The mate asked Steve.

Steve had just finished hanging up the phone with Sergeant Hernandez when the mate walked into the mess deck for a cup of coffee, after standing watch in the pilothouse.

Right then Sergeant Hernandez called again.

"That was quick," Steve said after answering the call. "I assume this is good news?"

"Not really," Hernandez said. "We did get an address, which led to a phone number. We called that number and it turned out to be a landline for an older woman in Merrillville, Indiana. That woman is the grandmother of this young man, and he has been living with her while going to college at the Purdue campus in Hammond. He uses her address for his credit card statements."

"Does the young man have a cell phone?" Steve asked.

"He does, and we've been calling that number, with no answer."

"And what about the young woman he was with?" Steve continued.

"The grandmother said the girl lived near the Purdue campus and had two roommates, in a private home, in which they rented a basement apartment. She gave us the young woman's name, but she had no phone number. We're working on that right now, and we'll update you again in about 45-minutes.

It was now almost 1 a.m., and Steve decided to call and update his father on the situation. Placing the call on speakerphone so the mate could hear the conversation, Steve told Curt everything that had happened since their last call, emphasizing that they now may have three, possibly four missing persons.

"Well, I'm going to head down to East Chicago. I can't sleep anyway, and my tossing and turning has just kept your mom awake," Curt said to Steve. "It's only about a 3-½ hour drive down there."

"No, you're not, big guy!" Steve heard his mom's voice say. "I'm not letting you drive alone, with no sleep. I'm going along to keep you awake!"

"What about the twins? I don't want them along in that neighborhood," Curt said.

"The grandparents are always complaining that they never get to see them. I'll call your parents and mine right now, explain the situation, and have them tag-team the two of them. They'll be thrilled."

"I guess you heard the boss, guys. That'll add about 30-minutes to drop off the twins, so we should be there about 7, Chicago time. That tug has enough staterooms, if I remember, so your mom and I will stay aboard until we decide what happens next."

"Great, Dad. Thanks for coming," said Steve. "So, you don't want me to get a hotel for you two?"

"Not yet. Hopefully, we find Ashley and Adam soon. If not, I'll see if Stormi can come over. She's off right now, but I hope she can take the tug if needed."

"Okay, Dad. See you soon. Looking forward to seeing you and Mom."

Chapter 3

TREVOR JORDAN

The man was a good-looking black man with graying hair. Steve guessed him to be about 50-years old. Steve and the tug's mate had been discussing their concerns when they heard a car horn and saw the lights shining through the mess deck porthole. When Steve stuck his head out the galley door, he saw the man standing next to the tug.

Now aboard the tug, the man introduced himself as Trevor Jordan, a driver for Uber. He said he had picked up two people at the tug the night before and driven them to Paisanos in Hammond.

"I got home and spoke to my wife after my shift, and she said the police had called, and that those two people were now missing. Are they okay?" the man continued.

Steve filled Mr. Jordan in on the situation.

"I remember that young couple in the restaurant," Trevor said after hearing Steve's account of what had happened. "Nice looking white couple, probably early twenties. They would not have caused any trouble for your friends. I didn't see any troublemakers in the place. Whatever happened probably occurred after they left. I really liked your friends and they treated me like I was a friend. I don't get that very often in this neighborhood."

Steve then suggested that Trevor call the police in case they had any questions for him. Steve showed Trevor the card from Sergeant Hernandez, and he made the call right away. Steve could tell that the police were asking the same questions he had already given them answers to, but then they must have asked why Mr. Jordan had not answered his phone.

"I don't like drivers who are always on the phone, and Uber doesn't want us to be distracted while driving. So, unless I recognize a call coming from my wife, I don't answer. If you had told my wife to call me, she would have told me to call you. I'm sorry, but she never called me to tell me about you calling."

The police must have said they didn't tell his wife it was urgent, because, at the time, it didn't appear to be a serious situation. Mr. Jordan said, "Next time you need to talk to me, tell Alma it's important!"

When Trevor hung up, he looked at Steve and said, "I don't know if that was any help, but I feel just terrible that your friends are missing. I asked them if I could wait and bring them back here when the pizzas were done, but they knew I was getting ride requests from Uber and said they'd make another Uber request when it was time to leave. I want to help in any way I can. What would you like me to do?"

"Are you sure, Trevor? It is great of you to offer," Steve said.

"Yes, please let me help."

"Well, the mate and I are stuck on the tug until my dad arrives from Michigan. What do you think we should do? We don't know the area, and we've never had this kind of trouble before."

"Maybe there's a way we can find the young couple who offered them a ride? I don't see that your friends would have attracted any trouble, but maybe the young couple has made some enemies, seeing they attend Purdue there in Hammond."

"We don't know much about them, but Sergeant Hernandez told us the young man lives with his grandmother in Merrillville, and his girlfriend lives in a basement apartment in Hammond with a couple of roommates. We don't know their names, but maybe the police will help. They found his name from the manager at Paisano's."

"I doubt the police will give out that information this early, but I know the manager at Paisanos. I think he'll help us if I call him," Trevor said.

"I don't know how receptive he'll be if you call him at this time of the morning."

"Jake's a good guy. I'll start out by apologizing for the early hour. I think my wife knows his wife, and I'm hoping she has their number." So, Trevor called his wife for a phone number.

"It's Jake's wife's cell phone, so I hope she doesn't turn it off at night, but let's give it a try," Trevor said after calling his wife and getting Jake's number.

Trevor was just about to hang up when we heard a sleepy woman's voice on the phone. Trevor said, "Doris, this is Trevor Jordan. I'm so sorry to be calling this time of the morning, but this is really important. Can I please speak to Jake?"

It took a couple of minutes before the man came to the phone. "Trevor, I assume you're calling about that couple you brought to the restaurant. They haven't found them?" Jakes's sleepy voice responded.

"No, they haven't. When I got home and heard what happened, I came down to the tug where I picked them up. I spoke with the police, but they're following all their rules, which will take too long. I didn't see any troublemakers in your place last night, and the tug people weren't the type to attract problems, so I'm guessing the young couple may have some local enemies. What do you think? Have you seen them before?"

Jake answered, "Sure. As I told the police when they called, his name is Bill Barnes. The girl is Julie Timms. They come in a couple times a month, and they seem fine. Bill's a nice kid. However, the girl has a couple roommates who occasionally come in for pizza. I don't like those two other girls, because they're loud and always bragging about their sleeping around. One time they came in with Julie, and I could tell that Julie was embarrassed by their talk. I heard them tell Julie she should dump Bill because he's a dork. They used much worse terms than that, but Doris is sitting right here. I told Julie that finding a good guy was tough, so if she liked Bill, she should hang onto him."

"So, it's possible those roommates could be involved here?"

"They weren't here last night, but they rent an apartment with Julie just two blocks down the street. Maybe Julie's roommates saw them leave the restaurant. I heard Bill offer the tug couple a ride, and I was happy because Bill's a responsible sort. I just hope they didn't run into some toughs out on the street."

"Do you know the address of Julie's apartment, Jake?"

"No, but I can describe it easy enough. It's south on Calumet, near that liquor store. It's the only house on that block with a basement apartment. An old couple owns the house, and they live on the first floor. They stopped in for pizza one time and Julie and Bill came in and sat with them. Julie introduced them as her landlords."

"Jake, you've been a great help. I'm going to run by that house and see if anyone's home."

"Darn, Trevor. I'm impressed that you're doing this. Please let me know what happens," Jake said.

"I'll be sure to keep you in the loop, Jake. The tug couple was just such nice, down-to-earth people, I can't just walk away from this. I want to be sure they're okay."

"Good luck, Trevor."

Steve looked at the mate. They were amazed at the progress Trevor had made in just a few minutes on the phone. "Darn, Trevor. You should be a private investigator," Steve said.

"Well, I've lived in this area my entire life. People know me, and that I take life seriously. Jake's wife and my wife volunteer at the same food pantry, so I knew that Jake would trust me asking questions."

"It was like watching a TV private eye in action," Steve said.

"Thanks, Steve. But I was serious about going to Julie's apartment to see if anyone knows where your two friends might be."

"I don't want you going there alone, Trevor. If something bad has happened, you could be walking into something dangerous, and I don't want your safety on my conscience."

Steve's phone rang just then. It was Curt. "Hey, it's my dad!" he said to Trevor. Then speaking into the phone, said, "Dad, I'm going to put you on speaker. We have some new developments you need to hear about."

Steve told Curt about Trevor and his conversation with the pizza place manager, and his desire to go to the girl's apartment. He also told Curt that he hated to see Trevor go there alone, and Curt agreed.

"Why don't you just call the police and give them this information?" Curt said.

Trevor answered, "Mr. Curt, I do like the local Police, but with their red tape, it might take them 24 hours to get there with a warrant, and it's in Hammond, out of their jurisdiction. If something bad happened, we don't want to wait that long."

"I understand, Trevor. I'd called to say I was just one hour away, but after our talk, I'm just over 30-minutes out. Steve can take care of the tug, and you and I can go to that apartment together."

"Dad," Steve interrupted. "I'm going along too. The Mate and three deckhands will be here, and Mom will also be on the tug. I've been too involved in this to stay behind."

"Okay! I guess your mom and I raised you right. The three of us will go. But whatever we find, we then turn this over to the local police. See you guys in a few minutes. Tell the mate to keep the tug safe and stand a radio watch. We'll call his cell phone with updates, and your mom can keep Uncle Bill informed."

Curt arrived thirty minutes later, just as he had said. Steve approached his father's truck and hugged and kissed his mother, Lois. Lois had spent the last ten years on and around tugboats, so she knew how to handle the situation. Trevor said he'd lead the way in his car, and Curt and Steve would follow in the truck. It was a busy morning and traffic slowed them down, but twenty minutes later, they were pulling up in front of the house which was assumed to be Julie Timms' apartment.

Trevor met Curt and Steve by his car and said, "How do we want to handle this? We're going to ask this old couple for information about a disappearance, but they'll know we aren't cops. I suggest one of you do the talking."

Curt gave Trevor a serious guy's side-hug and squeezed his shoulders. "I think you're the local team member on this investigation we have going here. You do the talking, and I'll only open my mouth if they don't seem to understand." That seemed to get a big smile on Trevor's face, and he led the way up to the door.

Three men standing on their doorstep, early on a Saturday morning, brought the older gentleman to the door with a very quizzical look on his face. And yes, the gentleman was very white. He asked, "How can I help you, gentlemen? You look like cops, but I don't see you flashing any badges."

Trevor asked him if Julie Timms rented his basement apartment, and if she had two roommates? At this, the old gentleman said, "Well, seeing you seemed to admit not to be policemen, I'm not sure that I should be divulging personal information."

Trevor then gave the man a brief description of the previous night's events, that Julie and her boyfriend, Bill, had offered a ride back to the tugboat for the crew members, after meeting them at Paisano's, and that the crew members never returned to their tug. Trevor then introduced Curt and Steve, including their relationship to the tugboat.

Looking Trevor in the eye, the astute gentleman asked, "And just how are you involved, sir?" Trevor explained that he was the Uber driver who drove the two from the tug to Paisano's, and he was worried when the East Chicago Police called him looking for information.

"Gentlemen, my name is Sam Snead, no relation to Sam, the golfer. He would not claim me as a relative if he saw my golf game. I can see that you are all serious, honest fellas, and are on a noble quest. Please come in and let me find my keys for the basement apartment."

Trevor smiled at Curt and Steve as Mr. Snead turned. All seemed to assume that Sam had used the golfing reference many times in his life. They then followed Mr. Snead into his home, where he introduced them to his wife, Dorothy. "Dotty, these gentlemen are look-ing for two overdue mariners, part of a tug crew down in Indiana Harbor. They were last seen with Julie, our downstairs tenant, and young Bill, her boyfriend."

Mrs. Snead asked her husband, "Have you told them of our concerns yet, Sam?"

"Not yet, Dotty. But here goes. Fellas, as you ap-peared on our doorstep, Dotty and I were discussing whether or not we needed to call the police. We heard a lot of commotion downstairs last night, around 9 o'clock. There was yelling and we think some furni-ture was broken, and then Dotty thought she heard someone making sounds like they were in pain. My hearing isn't what it used to be, so I missed that part of the commotion. But Dotty said the noises stopped abruptly, and we both heard the doors being slammed, and some female voices laughing and giggling. Then a loud car engine started and drove away. With you fellas showing up, and with the story you told me, I think we need to take a look in the basement. Would you agree?"

Trevor said, "Oh, yes. Please lead the way, Mr. Snead."

"Just Sam is fine. And may I call you Trevor?"

"Of course."

Sam led the way out the back door, to a side entrance that led to the basement apartment. Sam explained that although many cities ban basement apartments, Chicago and many surrounding municipalities had numerous older homes, originally built in the 1800s, with basement apartments. The safety code requirements are strict, but numerous such apartments exist.

Sam saw that the door wasn't locked, and he motioned for the other men to enter, he would follow. Sam seemed to be afraid of what they might find. The first thing they saw upon entry was the kitchen. Two wooden chairs were tossed upside down, feet apart from the small kitchen table as if they had been tossed in a scuffle. One chair had a broken leg. Minor traces of blood could be seen on the kitchen floor. In the large living area, there was a small, but obvious bloodstain on the carpet, next to a broken end table, near an old sofa.

Trevor said, "Something bad went down in here last night."

After he spoke, they all heard a muffled groaning

sound coming from one of three closed doors off the living room. They all turned, and Steve ran to the door and opened it.

"It's Adam!" Steve yelled. "He's tied to the bed and gagged."

The other three men followed Steve into the room, which was stifling hot. The room vents from the air conditioning had been closed as if done on purpose. Steve removed the gag from Adam's mouth and Adam immediately started shouting while gasping for air, "They took Ashley and Julie!"

"Who, where? Do you know who took them and where?" Steve asked Adam while trying to untie him.

Adam shook his head. "Bill is in bad shape, have you found Bill?"

Curt ran to open the other two doors while Steve finally got the rope loose on Adam's wrists.

"I found him," Curt shouted from one of the now open doors. "I think he's unconscious."

"I think it's time you call the Hammond Police and tell them we need an ambulance," Trevor said, turning to Sam Snead who looked stricken by the horror that was unfolding in his basement apartment.

"And you'd better tell them to contact the East Chicago Police because there is already an open, missing person case on these same people over there."

Chapter 4

ADAM

The sound of sirens blared in the close distance to everyone's relief. Bill lay spread out near the room where Curt had found him. They had agreed not to move him, and they would let the paramedics handle things.

Adam was now untied and pacing the living room. He was glad to see Curt and Steve Steiner and surprised to see their Uber driver, Trevor. Trevor had wanted to wait for him and Julie at the pizza place, and maybe he should have taken him up on that offer. But Ashley hated to see Trevor losing jobs while waiting for them, and they figured when they ordered another Uber ride back to the tug, Trevor might get the call again anyway.

"So, what happened," Curt asked Adam.

Adam told them he was very worried about Ashley, and Bill's girlfriend, Julie. But first, they had to get Bill to the hospital. He described how Bill had fought their abductors like a wild man, and how the men had pistol-whipped Bill pretty bad. When Adam went to help Bill, one of Julie's roommates hit Adam over the head with something. He said it couldn't have been the two men who were with the girls because both guys were standing in front of him when he got hit, so it had to be one of the girls.

He kept hammering on the point that Ashley and Julie had been taken by the two men and that something very fishy was going on with Julie's two roommates. They appeared to be friends with the two guys. Adam said that he was never totally unconscious, so after they tied him to the bed, he tried to listen closely to what was said, knowing that struggling to get loose would do him no good, and probably just get him shot.

Adam said he had heard enough details to know that these guys were working for some seriously bad people. He furiously called the guys *young punks* who looked like they had nothing to lose, which made them quite dangerous. He described how one of them had stopped the other from hitting Ashley when she hit one of the men.

"He said 'they' didn't pay as much for damaged goods."

"I wonder who 'they' are," Curt said.

"I think I might have an idea," Trevor chipped in. "There've been quite a few kidnappings and missing persons going on around here lately. I wonder if this is one such incident."

Just then, they heard the sirens in front of the

house and the sounds of quickening footsteps approaching the basement apartment. The Hammond Police were the first to arrive inside, followed right behind by three paramedics. Two of the paramedics carried a stretcher and placed it beside Bill, while the other bent over Bill to check his pulse and breathing. They found a faint pulse and placed Bill onto the stretcher.

Meanwhile, the police were speaking to Adam trying to get a statement.

As the police started to question Adam, he broke down. "First of all, my wife and Julie, Bill's girlfriend, have been kidnapped or abducted, if that's a better term. You have to get your people started on looking for them before we take any more time with questions."

"We'll get to that," the older policeman said, "but first we need to get details on what happened to you guys in this apartment."

"*That is* the story!" Adam yelled. "They took Ashley and Julie. It seems to be some trafficking thing. After they tied me to the bed, I heard them talking about selling the girls to some guy from Kentucky. You have to start looking for them right away."

"Okay! I'll have Les call it in while I get the details. What are their names?"

"My wife is Ashley Walters, and Bill's girlfriend is Julie. I'm not sure of her last name."

"It's Julie Timms," Trevor said.

"Thanks, Trevor. You're my hero, you know! When

Ashley is back safe, we really owe you, big time," Adam said to Trevor.

The older police officer continued to question Adam. "Who abducted them, and any idea of what they were driving? I need something to put on the bulletin otherwise we don't know who or what we're looking for."

"Two guys, late twenties or early thirties, both big guys. One had a short beard, not trimmed, and both had tattoos on their arms. The tattoos didn't all look professional, like maybe done by a friend. We saw an old, beat-up, white van on the street when we came, and I assume it was theirs. I remember seeing a lot of heavy rust around the rear wheel wells. I heard them start up when they left, and the van was very noisy. I think it has a bad muffler, and I also heard a heavy rattling noise as they pulled away. That muffler is probably loose, banging on the undercarriage."

Mr. Snead spoke up, "I also heard that noisy car. It was about 2 a.m. and it woke me up. My wife heard it too."

"Okay, Les. Step out the back door and call it in. Tell our Watch Commander we'll get more details to him soon. And they have about a four-hour head start." He then turned back to Adam, "But you mentioned Kentucky. What did they say about Kentucky? First, give me a synopsis of what happened, and then I'll get those details."

So Adam told him what had happened.

"Ashley and I met Bill and Julie at Paisano's, just up

the street, and Bill offered to give us a ride back to our tug, down in Indiana Harbor. Bill had parked his car here at Julie's apartment, so we walked here to get the car. That's when I saw the beat-up white van. It was getting a little chilly, so Julie said she wanted to grab her jacket from her apartment. Ashley and I stayed outside with Bill."

"So, you didn't come inside?" the policeman asked.

"I'm just getting to that. Julie went inside and I heard two other female voices, sounding quite drunk, and they were laughing, and talking trash to Julie. Then we heard Julie scream, 'No!' and then she said, 'Let me go.' That's when Bill, Ashley, and I went inside. We thought there were just the two drunk girls with Julie, but then we saw a bearded guy holding Julie and another one standing in front of her. The second guy said, 'Well, lookie here. We got a second young chick to deliver.' I told the guys to let Julie go, and we'd just leave. The second guy grabbed Ashley's arm, and Ashley hit him with her elbow. I think she may have broken his nose because blood was really flowing. That's when Bill rushed the guy holding Julie, and the second one pulled a gun out and started beating up on Bill. I told him to knock it off and I went to pull Bill away from the beating. One of those two girls must have hit me with something, and then they tied me to the bed and gagged me. I came around while they were tying me, but I kept my eyes closed and listened."

"And now tell me about the Kentucky thing. How do you know that?"

"As I was tied to the bed, I heard Ashley trying to reason with them. The non-bearded one must have been ready to hit Ashley for breaking his nose, because the other guy said, 'Don't hit her. Remember the guys in Kentucky pay less if they're marked up.' Then Ashley said, 'What are you talking about? We can't go to Kentucky.' The guy told her, 'Too late now chickie. You'll be in their stable this time tomorrow, and we'll get another $2500 for you. So, a nice five-Gs for one night's work.'"

"So, were they bringing all four women to Kentucky?" the policeman asked.

"I realized after listening to the four of them talk, that Julie's roommates were accomplices, not hostages. I could tell from the conversation that Julie didn't consider them friends, but they had probably lured her into their apartment with low monthly rent and were setting her up for these guys to kidnap her. It sounded like it had happened before."

"I think that those two girls are the first ones we need to find. What did they plan on doing with you and the other fella, Bill?"

"I believe they were going to come back here after they delivered Ashley and Julie. They didn't plan on us being here, so I don't think they knew what to do with us. These guys are not pros, just a couple tough guys, morons really. I started thinking they were just going to dump us in the Canal tonight, hoping we had both died down here. I even heard them say, 'Shut off the AC. That'll do it.'"

"I'm sure those two girls are spooked over what went down. Can you describe them?" the policeman asked?

Again, Mr. Snead spoke up, "I can do better than that, officer. I have pictures of the two girls, and I might want to give you the names and pictures of others they have shared the apartment with. I always keep that information with my renters' contracts."

"That's fantastic, Mr. Snead. Please get them for me. And Mr. Walters, do you have a picture of your wife?"

"Well, they took my wallet, but I do have a picture back on the tug."

"Sergeant, are you going to call the State Police?" Trevor asked. "If that van is on its way to Kentucky, the State boys could be watching for it on I-65, right?"

"We know how to handle these things," the Sergeant answered, obviously irritated.

"Just sayin'. Louisville is only four hours away, but I'm hoping that old van gave them trouble. And if they intended to enter Kentucky, isn't this also an FBI kidnapping case?"

"I need to call the station with this further information. Excuse me."

It was obvious this guy didn't like being told how to do his job. But Curt, Steve, and Adam all grinned at Trevor.

Curt said, "I think you're starting to irritate this sergeant, Trevor. Not sure if that's a good idea."

"I don't think too much of the Hammond cops, Curt. As soon as he's done asking questions, I'm going to call Sergeant Hernandez, over in East Chicago. That may be a smaller town than Hammond, but Hernandez takes his job more seriously. Seeing he filed some kind of missing person report last night on Adam and his wife, he will still consider this his responsibility."

"I also didn't get a good feeling from this guy," Adam said. "He seems more worried about Bill and me getting beat up than he is about finding Ashley and Julie. I want to do something myself, but I don't know where to start."

"Let's ask this sergeant if he's done with us, and let's try to find Sergeant Hernandez," Steve said. "I was impressed with him last night when he came to the tug."

Just then, the Sergeant came back into the apartment and said, "Okay. I have your statements and contact information. We'll call you if anything develops. Will you all be in the area if we need to contact you?"

Steve looked at Curt with a questioning look and Curt said, "Yes, we'll be available. I'll be staying at the Best Western over here on Calumet Avenue as well as Mr. Walters and my son. The tug may need to leave later today."

"Fine. We'll be in contact. Thank you," the Sergeant said.

Curt, Adam, Steve, and Trevor thanked Mr. Snead

for his cooperation on their way out of the apartment. The ambulance had already left, followed by the sergeant and his men from the Hammond police department.

"I should have known those two girls were trouble," Mr. Snead said, as the men walked back up to the main floor of the building. He seemed to still be getting over the fact that he had rented space in his home to criminals.

Trevor patted Mr. Snead on his back, reassuringly. None of them were judging him.

"Dotty told me we should have called the police because of their loud parties, but I never did. I had no idea that the string of those third renters was part of some illegal scheme to kidnap those girls."

"It's become a dangerous world, Sam. It's hard to keep up with everything these bad-ass opportunists are doing," Trevor said. "Don't feel guilty. It wouldn't be something you'd have suspected."

"I still feel just terrible that it happened right under our noses. If there's anything I can do, please call me."

"Well, for one thing, call the police if anyone comes back to the apartment, but would you also call one of us? And I'll have Sergeant Hernandez call you," Trevor said. "I think he'll want the names of these two girls, as well as those other girls who stayed with them in the apartment. I'm wondering if they'll turn out to be missing persons as well."

"I certainly will. And Adam, we sure hope they locate your wife and Julie, both safe and sound."

"Thanks," Adam said.

As the four men headed towards Curt's truck, Curt asked Adam if he wanted to stop over at the hospital to get the cut on his head checked out.

"No way, boss. I'm fine, and I just want to get the search started for Ash and Julie," Adam said. A cut could wait, finding his wife could not.

"Okay," Curt replied, before turning to Trevor. "What do you suggest we do next? I can see why you weren't happy with the way this sergeant reacted."

"I'll call Hernandez right now. I've known him for a long time, and he'll know what to do. He helped my son out of a jam when my son was in middle school. Follow me and we'll head back toward East Chicago, and I'll ask him to meet us."

When we arrived back at the tug in Indiana Harbor, Sergeant Hernandez was already on the dock, next to the tug, talking to Lois Steiner, Curt's wife.

"I thought we'd meet here," Hernandez said as the men approached the tug. "Trevor doesn't seem to think the Hammond guys are treating this abduction seriously, so for now, our talk will be off the record. Once I hear the whole story, we can decide what to do." He turned to Adam, "And you're Adam Walters? One of the missing people from my report last night? And your wife is still missing?"

"Yes, that's right. And I'm frustrated, wondering what we need to do next."

Hernandez nodded and assured Adam that he was on top of things.

"Steve, I just met your mother here. She speaks highly of you. Can we go aboard? I'm hoping you may have some strong coffee in the galley?"

"We sure can, Sergeant. And by the way, this is my dad, Curt Steiner. He's the Operations Manager for Strauss Marine Construction, so he's also my boss."

Curt squeezed Steve's shoulder and said, "Trevor has said good things about you, Sergeant. Good to meet you. Let's get aboard. I could use some coffee as well."

After Adam gave Sergeant Hernandez the full story, Hernandez suggested that he first call Mr. Snead. "I'd like to get all the names of the girls involved. Because one of them hit Mr. Walters, I will expand the case into assault, so we can also look for them as part of our case. Then get Julie Timms' details, of course. But I'm very worried about those other girls who stayed in that apartment. I think they may also have been abducted by these two guys. We've heard about the possibility of a trafficking ring in the area, but this is the first real clue we've found that one exists."

"Just what do you mean by 'trafficking', Sergeant?" Steve asked.

"Trafficking is the abduction of young women, and some young boys, who are sold into what they call stables. They are usually used for sexual purposes, both in this country, and some are even sold to other countries."

"Wouldn't some of the women and boys refuse to

cooperate? And why aren't the two girls who helped these thugs being used in those stables?" Steve asked.

"If they're unwilling to cooperate, which is probably true for most of them, they're either starved or drugged and maybe threatened in some way, until they cooperate. As for these two girls who are working with the abductors, I can assume they've lived on the rough side of life for too long. The clients in these stables are looking to have their way with young, innocent women and boys because they want to feel like they are taking advantage of them, which they are. Many times, when the women and boys become too hardened, they're sold overseas, or even killed."

"Really sick," Steve said.

"We need to find Ash before something terrible happens," Adam said. It was obvious that he was getting very emotional about Ashley's welfare.

"It certainly is sick. But now, let me make a call to a friend of mine with the State Police. I think we can still intercept that van, based upon Adam's description. He will also probably contact the FBI, because of the mention of crossing into Kentucky, although trafficking is a federal statute case anyway."

Sergeant Hernandez made the call to his friend with the State Police. After giving him the details, he told Sergeant Hernandez to sit tight for fifteen minutes, and he'd call him back. The entire group sat in the tug's mess deck, drinking coffee. Adam excused himself to change his bloodied shirt.

When Adam returned, Hernandez asked for Adam's shirt as evidence of his assault. A few seconds later, the Sergeant's phone rang. "Hi, Tom. That was quick," he said. And after a pause, he said, "No, it is Ashley Walters, not Rawlins."

"Wait," Adam yelled. "Ashley's maiden name is Rawlins. That's her!"

"Tom, did you hear that? That's her driver's license. Where was it found?" Again, after a long pause, "Okay, keep your guys on it, and please keep us well informed."

"Where is she?" Adam pleaded. He was a big, tough guy, but he had tears in his eyes.

"They haven't found Ashley, but it appears those guys are using back roads, staying off the Interstate. They gassed up in a small town, Russiaville, just east of Lafayette. It was one of those old, small service stations, the kind with the restrooms outside. They must have taken the girls to the restroom. This morning, while cleaning the restrooms, the employee found a driver's license sticking out the back side of the toilet paper dispenser. He thought it was unusual and called his local county police, and they called it in to the State because it was a Michigan license. It looks like your wife was thinking on her feet and hoped this might trigger a response. I'm surprised that she still had her license."

"Ashley didn't take a purse or a wallet along last night. She just stuck her driver's license in her pocket, to have an ID. Her license still has her maiden name because we've only been married a year. Spending most of our time on the tugs, we seldom need to drive, and I do most of the driving."

"Understood. You've got a great little lady there. And by the way, Tom is checking out the names of the other girls who rented in that apartment, in case they're also reported missing. He's also notified their investigators, with information on those two female accomplices. I'm betting they're still in the Hammond area and are now afraid to return to their apartment. I think they'll be apprehended quickly."

"What can we do to help?" Adam asked. "I can't just sit here and do nothing."

"I wish I could give you something more to do, but for now, just be ready to come when we call. We'll need you to identify those two girls when we locate them, and as soon as we find your wife, we'll get you to her as quickly as we can."

"Thank you, Sergeant. I just feel so helpless."

When Sergeant Hernandez left, Curt suggested that they check on how young Bill was doing at the hospital, then rent a car for Steve so he could drive Adam to Ashley as soon as they found her. He also suggested that they get a couple of rooms at the Best Western. "I'm going to call Captain Stormi and another engineer to take this equipment up to Traverse City. The crew needs these scows up there. I think the rest of us need to stay here until Ashley is found safe and sound."

"And what are we going to do with Trevor?" Adam

asked. "Without this man's concern, Bill and I would probably have died and been dumped somewhere."

"I put Trevor on our payroll about six hours ago, whether he likes it or not. He's now part of the Strauss Marine family!" Curt answered, smiling.

Chapter 5

ASHLEY

Damn! I can't believe what kind of trouble a couple pizzas has gotten us into. I'm really worried about Adam. I could tell he wasn't hurt too badly when that little bitch hit him with that cutting board, but I can hear these two goons talking, and they're really scared that Adam and Bill might be found before they get back to Hammond. If the guys are still in that apartment when they get back, I'm afraid of what they'll do to them.

Poor Julie is just plain freaked out. I keep whispering to her that we need to find ways to delay these guys, but she isn't thinking clearly. I can't talk much because the shitheads get upset when we talk. But at least I had those few minutes in that restroom, while they were gassing up the van. I hope someone responsible finds my driver's license and not some girl thinking she got lucky to get a false ID. I may look young because I'm so small, but I'm always questioned because nobody believes I'm 37.

Apparently, these two idiots have been taking young girls, who those two freaky broads have sub-leased into their apartment, and they're selling them to some kind of sex ring down in suburban Louisville. These guys are talking pretty freely up front, so when I get outa this mess, do I ever have a story to tell about this operation.

I'm whispering to Julie to get them to stop, saying she is car sick and needs to upchuck. I have a plan, but I need to get them to stop. I told her to be sure to go on the right side of the car because I want to be on the left. I'll tell them I need to get some fresh air before I get sick too. I just hope Julie can force herself to throw up and can keep their attention for a few minutes. I don't dare run because both of them have guns. I want to get out of this in one piece so I can see these assholes behind bars.

I finally get Julie to understand, and she's talking to the two guys up front. "If you don't pull over, I'm going to vomit right here on your back. I'm serious. Let me upchuck in the ditch and get some fresh air, and I'll be okay."

"Shit! Okay, Larry. We'd better pull off in a farmer's driveway. You keep an eye on the second one, and I'll watch this one spill her dinner."

"Can't you wait for a half-hour? We need to stop again to gas up."

"I'm ready to puke right now. I can't wait."

"Yeh, if she does it in here, it'll make me toss-up too. I see a quiet drive over there."

"Okay. You two have caused so much fuckin' trouble, I almost wish we hadn't snatched you."

This van appears to be an old cable company installer's vehicle. I can see where they had shelves or work areas inside, which have been torn out. There are no windows on the side or back, and the inside is rusting where the paint was chipped off. The floor has green carpeting, like that cheap, Indoor-outdoor stuff people put on their decks. It's covered with junk, dirty rags, old Burger King bags, and I see some old chicken bones in the mix. There would be nowhere to sit if it weren't for the spare tire back here, which is flat. Julie has been sitting on one side of the tire and me on the other, but when the guys take a sharp turn, one or both of us falls off onto the floor. I think they're taking those sharp turns purposely, just to see us fall off the tire.

While they're talking to Julie, I'm stuffing as many bottles of water into my jacket pockets as I can, being sure to break the seals beforehand. As I'm doing that, I also find a can of brake fluid amongst the junk in the back. I wonder if that will help to gum up the works? I'm glad they're low on gas, so my idea may work.

They pull off on a narrow side road. I can hear branches scrape along the side. Because the van only has windows in the front, and solid panels on the sides and rear doors, I can't tell if I'll have room to do what I want. They open the rear door and the bearded guy, I think is Henry, grabs Julie and she immediately heads to the right side. Good girl! I start to get out, but Henry says, "No you don't. Just her."

"I'm getting motion sick back here without any windows," I told him. I'll be the next one to be sick if I don't get some fresh air."

"Larry," he yells, "your buddy here needs some air. Jump out and keep an eye on her."

Larry is the one I clobbered in the nose. I'm hoping I might have broken it. That self-defense course has finally paid some dividends. So, Larry shuts off the van, jumps out, and wants to lead me over by Julie, who I can see has caused herself to get a little bile to come up. I said, "Not there. If I watch her, I'm sure to up-chuck." So, he pushes me around the back corner to the left side, where I feign a half faint, leaning against the side, over the gas tank. The door is missing, and I open the cap, then slowly start opening the bottles of water and dump them in. Larry is watching Julie and Henry around the back of the van. I get two bottles in then my hand finds the can of brake fluid, which I also dump into the tank. As I start to empty the third bottle of water, the can falls out of my pocket. Larry hears the clinking noise when the can hits the ground, and he notices what I've been doing.

"Damn you fuckin' bitch!" he yells. "What are ya'll doing?" He pulls me away and slugs me. I see stars, but don't pass out.

"Shit, Larry. I told you not to mark her up," Henry yells.

"I caught her trying to put water in the gas tank.

She already dumped a can of brake fluid in there. I'd kill this one if I could. First my nose, and now this."

"I don't think the brake fluid is a problem. And it looks like she didn't get the full bottle of water in there. We'll stop at the next gas station and fill up. That should take care of it. Just calm down."

"If you hadn't made us swing so far around Indianapolis, we'd be in Louisville by now."

"But if they're looking for us, they'll think we're taking the Interstate. Taking these side roads is safer."

"Okay, okay. Let's get these bitches back in the van and get moving." And with that, Larry picked my 100-pounds off the ground and threw me bodily into the back of the van, causing the left side of my face to get scratched up on the old tartan-turf stuff on the floor. At least it will balance off the quickly swelling right side, where he hit me.

In the back of the van, Julie sees my face and starts to cry. I calm her down and hand her a bottle of water and show her the two empty bottles the goons hadn't noticed. I ask her to try to clean any cuts with the water, which she does. I'm starting to see just how stupid these so-called crooks really are. That just may be a blessing, because if they really knew what they were doing, they would have searched my pockets and found my driver's license, and I'd never have gotten away with dumping shit in their gas tank. Meanwhile, I was disappointed that the van seemed to be running okay.

Then I started to hear Larry ask, "How far is it to

that North Vernon place? It seems like we're running out of gas."

I saw Henry look over and say, "Can't be. It's just below a quarter tank."

"Well, it's bucking some, like it does when it's almost empty."

"How much water did your honey get in the tank?"

"Just a half bottle. But I don't know how much was in that brake fluid can."

"We'd better get some gas to dilute that stuff. See that farm over there? Let's pull in and buy some from the farmer."

I could really feel the van chugging, so either the water, all 2-½ bottles, or possibly that brake fluid, were doing their job. They pulled into the farm driveway, and I heard Henry get out.

"Pull any fuckin' shit and I swear I'll kill one of you! Just stay back there on the floor," Larry warned us before following Henry out of the van.

Shortly thereafter, I heard Henry talking to the farmer, who said he could spare a few gallons. Henry thanked the farmer and asked if $10 would cover it. The farmer said alright, and then I heard a woman's voice, probably the farmer's wife, asking what was going on. I figured this might be the chance I was waiting for, but I didn't want the farmer and his wife to get hurt. I knew I had to be careful so I wouldn't be found out. When I was sure Henry and Larry would be distracted by the farmer as they gassed up the van, I peeked over the driver's seat. There was an old lady, maybe late 60s, with white hair in a bun, and a plain house dress standing near the front of the van. I made sure the two assholes couldn't see me and slowly waved my hand. I thought it wasn't working, but all of a sudden, the woman caught my movement and looked in my direction. She started to walk closer to the van, but I held up my hand, motioning her to stop. She looked surprised but played along very well when I slowly mouthed the words, CALL FOR HELP. She was close enough that I think she could see my face, so I turned to each side and pointed at my injuries. Then I motioned for her to leave. Not very long after our encounter, I heard the lady loudly say to Henry and Larry, "Good to meet you boys. Drive safe." I figured she had gotten the message.

"Good thing you girls stayed quiet. I'd have trouble controlling old Larry here. He's pretty upset about this gas thing," Henry said when they got back in the van.

I looked at Julie and chuckled. She smiled back weakly, still very afraid of what was to come. Then Henry tried to start the engine but was having trouble. The engine cranked up reluctantly after a few more tries and Henry backed the van out of the yard. Once we were moving, the engine seemed to run okay.

A few minutes later, we pulled into the service station at North Vernon, and Julie asked to go to the restroom again. Again, they made us go together, and

Henry stood outside the door. I found a broken eye-liner on the floor, and used it to write a message on the back of the door:

HELP – HELD CAPTIVE – CALL ADAM AT 231-555-4231 – FROM ASHLEY

I had thought of writing it on the mirror, but when Henry opened the door, he held the door open and looked around. He never thought to look at the back of the door. In my mind, I started calling them Moe & Larry. They sure were stupid enough.

Again, they had a hard time starting the van. My handy work seemed to be working. As we continued, I heard Moe, I mean Henry, say that this piece of shit van would never make it to Little Spring, and he'd hate to have trouble going through Louisville. He said, "Besides, if they're looking for this van, getting another one might be smart." That was the first time I heard the name Little Spring. I wondered where that was.

"Isn't there a big church on the other side of this town?" I heard Larry ask Henry. "I remember it from the last time we came this way. It's Saturday, so the parking lot should be full for afternoon services. If we get lucky, we can find another van," he continued.

Henry seemed to agree, because sure enough, a few minutes later, they found the church, but the parking lot was almost empty. I could tell they were roaming around the parking lot, looking for a car or van. Henry would hop out occasionally but come back in and say it was locked or too small. Then finally, they stopped again, and Henry said, "This one is locked, but I see a set of keys on the center console. Give me that pry-bar under the seat."

The next thing I know, they're throwing us in the back of the church's minibus. These morons were stealing a van with the name of the church on the side. This should be easy to spot. Then I also noticed that they didn't force a door, they had broken the window in the passenger boarding door. Despite our terrible circumstances, these idiots were giving us a chance.

Chapter 6

ADAM

It was tough enough sitting on the tug, waiting for a call from the police. The crew never heard anything from the Hammond Police, but at least Sergeant Hernandez was calling every hour, even if it was just to say he had no good news yet. Adam was so worried about Ashley. She may be a tough tugboat captain who takes no crap, but she was just a little slip of a thing. Those two goons were huge. If she mouthed off at them, which she occasionally does when she's upset, Adam worried they might hurt her.

Stormi Weaver arrived at the tug on Saturday afternoon with a deckhand to replace Steve. She would be replacing Ashley.

She immediately ran to up Adam when she arrived and, despite her tough exterior, she was crying.

"Oh God, Adam. Any word about Ashley yet? I can't believe all of this."

Stormi was a great captain with a lot of experience, both Great Lakes and deep sea. She was the captain who first broke in Ashley, starting to train her as a captain. Ashley was even the godmother to Stormi's and her partner's youngest adopted girl; that's how tight the two of them were.

"No good news yet Cap. Ash did plant her driver's license in a service station restroom. That's the only clue so far."

"She's a tough nut. Those guys will end up sorry they took her. She really thinks on her feet. And hey! I'm the one who trained her. Right?"

"I keep thinking that way. But I'm scared for her. These guys are more than just stupid, and they may do something bad if things go wrong."

Stormi was with Adam when he received the call from Sergeant Hernandez who said he had some hopeful news.

"They stopped at a farm near North Vernon, a small town, southeast of Lafayette. The farmer said they thought they were out of gas. But the good news is that his wife saw movement in the van, and a woman in the back mouthed the words, CALL FOR HELP, and then pointed to injuries on both sides of her face," Sergeant Hernandez told Adam.

"Damn them. They have hurt her. I had a feeling!"

"If it's any consolation, the farmer's wife said she didn't seem to be badly hurt. But the farmer only sold them three gallons, so he assumes they went to the small service station in town, and the State boys are sending a car down there now."

"She's still thinking on her feet. That's my girl!"

"That's right Adam. Keep thinking positive. She's doing all the right things."

"Thanks for the call, Sarge."

"See, I told you I trained her right," Stormi said, chuckling after Adam got off the phone.

Right then, Adam got another call from a number he didn't recognize.

"This is Adam. Can I help you?" he said, answering the call.

"Do you know someone named Ashley?" asked an older woman's voice.

"Yes, Ashley is my wife."

"Is she in some kind of trouble?"

"Yes, she was abducted. The police are looking for her."

"Well, I wanted to be sure. Someone wrote a message on the inside of the ladies' room door, in a gas station in Indiana. I was going to report it to the police, but first I wanted to be sure it wasn't a hoax."

"Oh, Ma'am, I can't thank you enough. Is it North Vernon? Give me the location and your name, so I can give it to the State Police. They're on their way to North Vernon now, because a farmer also saw my wife there. But please, also call the local police if you would. This is more good news. Thank you."

After they exchanged information, Adam called Sergeant Hernandez. He told Hernandez about the message in the restroom.

"I'm glad you called, Adam. Two good pieces of information. The State guys went to North Vernon and spoke with the farmer and his wife. They then went to the gas station in town. The mechanic definitely remembers those two guys, and he said their van sounded terrible when it started up. One of the officers was a woman, and she used the restroom at the station. She saw the same message from your wife on the back of the door."

"That's all very wonderful news, but Ash is still in trouble."

"That's true, but with the way your wife keeps coming up with ideas, I have a very good feeling that she is a survivor."

"Hey, Sarge. I have a call coming in from Trevor. Can I call you back?"

"Sure. Knowing him, he's probably found something."

Adam took Trevor's call, "Hey there. Did you get some sleep?"

"Well, I first led Curt and Steve to the hospital to check on Bill. They're keeping Bill sedated, but he will survive. He has a couple small skull fractures, so they are going to send him to a Chicago hospital, with better access to specialists. Curt and Steve then went out to visit Bill's Grandma. She doesn't drive and only has a landline, so they wanted to keep her posted. But here is some great news."

"Good. I've also had some good news from Sergeant Hernandez. They know where Ash and Julie have been, but they haven't found them yet. What's your news?"

"While I was driving to the hospital, I got an Uber request. I turned it down, but it got me thinking. Those two girls who set up Julie, can't go to their apartment, and apparently, they don't have a car. I figured they were Uber people. Uber won't release personal info, even to drivers, but I personally know most of the drivers in the area. I started calling them, and sure enough, a lady driver, Betty Hermans, remembered two girls as I described, and she remembered where she dropped them off. It's a house over in Black Oak, not far from Hammond. I'll bet it's where those two creepy guys also live."

"Oh, that's just fantastic, Trevor. You really are a detective. Shall we call Sergeant Hernandez or the Hammond cops?"

"Let me call Hernandez. He'll probably pass it on to his buddy with the State. I still think that Hammond guy will screw this up."

"I agree, Trevor. You call the Sarge, seeing you have all the information. Let me know what he plans to do. And Trevor, thank you so much! I'm not sure where we would be without your help."

"I've been helped throughout my life. I'm just paying it forward."

Chapter 7

LOUIS HERNANDEZ

The way Louis Hernandez tells it: before he was Sergeant Hernandez, he was the son of a laborer. His father was born in Texas to Mexican farmworkers. When he was nineteen, he heard about the good pay at the Indiana steel mills and made his way north where he got a laborers job in the mills. He was a good worker and was promoted often. It was at the steel mills that his father met his mother. His father loved to tell the story about how they met. He was leaving work one day when he bumped into a lady and apologized for nearly tripping her. Instead of being upset, the woman simply smiled and said it was okay.

Hernandez's father detected an accent when the woman spoke and assumed she was from Poland.

"No, not from Poland," the woman responded kindly. "I'm from Hungary...Hungarian."

His father laughed. If you're hungry, can I buy you dinner?"

The lady looked shocked and said, "No, I am from the country called Hungary."

Hernandez's father again apologized, and they started to see one another. Six months later, they were married. And two years later, their first child, Louis Hernandez, was born. His parents had since been married for over 46-years and have three other children.

Louis joined the East Chicago Police Department eighteen years ago. Before then, he worked in the steel mill for a few years. He started on a beat but was taking college courses at night, including courses in Criminal Justice. Hernandez soon made Sergeant and was now next in line for an Inspector's badge, a plain-clothes guy.

East Chicago is a tough, steel mill town, with a lot of seedy bars, but there are also a lot of honest, hard-working people who live there in nice neighborhoods. One such honest, hardworking guy was Trevor Jordan.

Hernandez had known Trevor Jordan for maybe ten or twelve years. When Trevor's son, Eldon, was caught with some guys who had broken into a convenience store to steal cigarettes, when he was only thirteen, it was Hernandez who took Eldon home to discuss the situation with his father. Eldon had said he wasn't involved with the break-in, but he was smoking the stolen cigarettes with the boys that did. Hernandez believed him because the kid was very contrite. After presenting Trevor with the facts, Hernandez had expected Trevor to start defending his son, or worse, start beating the kid in front of him. He'd seen both scenarios occur. Instead, Trevor spoke to Eldon in a way he'd rarely seen parents speak to their children.

"I've told you not to hang with those guys, son. Trouble is like shit, Eldon. It sticks to you, and you can't get rid of the smell."

The boy's face looked like he'd been beaten, and Hernandez could see that the boy respected his dad. The verbal reprimand seemed to mean more to him than a beating would have.

Hernandez sat for over ten minutes listening to the boy's apologies and Trevor giving sincere, fatherly advice. Then Trevor said, "Officer, what would you like me to do with this young man?" As a police officer, he'd never been asked that by a parent before, and all he could say was, "Do you have any suggestions? I want him to learn from this."

Trevor said, "Do you have any service projects that Eldon can do? Something where he can learn responsibility, and hard work? Keep him busy after school?"

"My mom is a nurse over at the Nursing Home a few blocks from here," Hernandez said after giving it some thought. "She always talks about needing volunteers to run errands for the 'old people', as she calls them. Some don't have family nearby, and they sometimes just need a friend. Someone to talk to, and maybe read to them. How does that sound?"

"Maybe throw in some raking the yard, picking up

trash, and anything else that needs to get done, and that sounds like a good deal. What do you think, Eldon?" Trevor said.

"I think I'd like that," Eldon said.

"Maybe it's too cushy then, so tell your mom to throw in some dishes, maybe even some bedpans," Trevor responded.

Hernandez looked over at Eldon and saw a hidden smile on his face, which he interpreted as respect for his father. They made the deal, and the next day Sergeant Hernandez introduced Eldon to his mom. After a few months, Eldon was visiting most rooms every day, the 'inmates', as my mom referred to them, looked forward to Eldon's visits. He read to them, and he even learned to juggle and did some simple magic tricks he learned from a library book, just to see the smiles on their faces. And yes, Mrs. Hernandez occasionally made him rake and pick up trash, but no bedpans.

After three months, Sergeant Hernandez visited Trevor again and met his wife, Alma. During that visit, he told them Eldon had done a great job and was free from restitution. Trevor looked over at Eldon. Louis Hernandez could tell that Trevor was proud of his son.

"Officer Hernandez, would it be okay with your mom if I kept going in to see her and her 'inmates'? They've all become my friends, and they would miss me if I stopped coming," Eldon said.

Hernandez looked over at Trevor, and the pride on his face was beautiful to see. He even saw a tear in Alma's eye.

"I'm sure my mom would love to have you stop by, but just when you have time. I don't want you to let this get in the way of your studies, or chores for your parents."

"I can work that out, Officer Hernandez. A couple of the 'inmates' used to teach school, and they offered to help me with my math and science. They also ask me to read books for them that are really interesting. And your mom sneaks me extra desserts, but I'm not supposed to tell."

"If it's okay with your mom and dad, it's just fine with me."

Eldon visited the nursing home probably four days a week, all the way through high school. He became a pretty good juggler, and his magic wowed the residents. The staff threw birthday parties for him each year, and many of the families of the residents gave him gifts at Christmas. Eldon even attended funerals for every one of his 'friends' who died during the years he was there. When he went away to college, he still went back to visit when he could.

Hernandez's respect for Trevor never ceased after his experience with Eldon, which made his involvement in the abduction case even more remarkable. Trevor cared about people, even his Uber passengers, and he considered their welfare to be his responsibility.

Therefore, when Trevor called Hernandez with information about the two girls suspected to be involved with the abduction, and possibly others, Sergeant Hernandez was eager to know what had been found.

"Louis, I think we found those two girls. Betty Hermans, I think you know her, had an Uber ride for two girls that matched the description I gave her. She dropped them at a house out in Black Oak. I'm betting those two suspects with the van live out there. Betty said it was a real shack."

"Did you call Hammond with this, Trevor?"

"No way. I don't want them to screw this up," Trevor said.

"Off the record, I'm glad you didn't. I'm going straight to the State Police with this information. Give me the address and I'll call right away. And thank you, Trevor."

Within two hours, the two female suspects were in custody. The State police asked both the East Chicago and Hammond Police to be at their interrogation. They also had Adam watch them through the one-way mirrors, and he identified them as the girls who were helping the abductors. The girls were interrogated separately and at first, both of them said they had no idea what the investigator was talking about. "Funny, because this abduction went down in your apartment, and the big guy you hit with the cutting board gave us a perfect description of you." One of the girls, Trisha, said, "It was Darlene who hit him!" then she realized what she'd said and so decided to keep talking.

The second girl, Darlene, faced a jail term just for the assault, but the investigator told her that this had become an FBI kidnapping because they were crossing state lines with their captives. She would probably spend years in Federal prison. When she heard that, she broke down. "It's Henry and Larry's deal. We don't know anything about it," she confessed.

"But you left two seriously wounded men in your apartment to die. You're both accessories to quite a string of charges."

"What if I cooperate, can I get off?"

"Not totally, but it could make a difference in the judge's sentencing."

"Okay. I'll tell you what I know," she said.

"First, I need to know where they're taking them?"

"To some church around Louisville. I don't know where, but I think Trisha knows. Larry told her last time." Again, Darlene realized that she had involved herself in the previous abduction, and she dropped her eyes to the table.

Thank God some criminals are so dumb, Hernandez thought.

The interrogator went back to the room where Trisha was being held and told her everything Darlene had said. "Stupid bitch," she mumbled.

"So, if you cooperate, it may help you as well. Darlene said you know the name of the church they're heading to in Louisville. It will help you if you cooperate."

"It's not in Louisville. It's a small town called Little Spring. He never told me the name of the church."

Armed with this new information, the State Police

informed Adam of further information they had been withholding. . They had a lead investigator who now wanted to speak with Ashley Walters' husband.

The State investigator, a nice man called Norman Jenkins, wanted to arrange a meeting with Adam, so Hernandez asked Mr. Jenkins to meet him and Adam aboard the tugboat in Indiana Harbor, and he agreed.

When Jenkins and Hernandez arrived at the tug, it was obvious that Norman Jenkins had never been on a working vessel before. He wasn't scared, but his eyes darted everywhere, trying to take in all the unusual details. Hernandez hadn't been on too many ships and tugs either, but working around Indiana Harbor, he was certainly more familiar than Norman was.

Sergeant Hernandez introduced Mr. Jenkins to Curt, Steve, Lois, Adam, and the few deckhands who were in the galley finishing their meals.

"Mr. Jenkins, we could move up to the pilothouse to talk if you'd like," Curt said. "The galley is a bit busy at mealtime. Who would you like to have involved in your discussion? Just so you know, I'm the Operations Manager for the company, Lois is my wife, as well as the niece of the owner, and Steve is my son. Steve was aboard when Adam and Ashley disappeared, and he's the one who raised the first alarm that something was wrong."

"Seeing each of you has some knowledge of the situation, I think it would be good to have all of you in this conversation." Then looking over at the two deck-hands, Jenkins added with a smile on his face, "You guys are excused though. You can finish your meal. It smells good, by the way!"

"I think it's just sloppy joe," Adam said.

They all headed up to the pilothouse where Captain Stormi was planning her voyage to Traverse City, and Mr. Jenkins started to talk. "First of all, Mr. Walters, your wife is safe and sound. We have the two men in custody, but they're refusing to cooperate. We have an idea of how to proceed, but your wife, one heck of a brave lady, said we needed to get your permission before going ahead with the plan."

"So, Ashley's okay? I'm so relieved. Is she hurt at all?"

"It looks like one of the suspects may have hit her, one side of her face is swollen. The other side of her face is scratched, where she said she scraped her face on the van's carpet when they threw her in the back. We wanted to take her to the hospital, but she refused. And she was happy to hear that you were not badly hurt."

"Damn those guys! I can't wait to get my hands on them. Where are they?"

"You may get to see them again," Jenkins said. "I can't promise you any close contact, but stranger things have happened."

"And how is the young girl, Julie?"

"She seems quite traumatized but is physically okay.'

"And just how did you find them?" Adam asked.

"I can hardly believe this story. As I said, your wife

is very brave, but she has a built-in survivor's instinct. You already know about her leaving her driver's license in the restroom, and later getting the attention of the farmer's wife to call for help. And in that case, she could have jumped out of the van or had the woman come to the van, but she stopped her, not wanting her captors to hurt them."

"Yes, that's Ash. Always thinking."

"Then she left that message in the next rest stop, and the lady who found that called you, I understand. But this is the new information we came across, which you haven't heard. Your wife talked the young girl, Julie, into faking being sick, and when the men pulled over onto a side road, to let the girl vomit, your wife acted faint and fell against the car. In that position, she was able to dump two bottles of water and a can of brake fluid into the gas tank before they caught her. That's when one of the men hit her and threw her into the back of the van."

"I hope I can get my hands on those guys," Adam said, pounding his fist hard into the palm of his hand.

"Maybe we can arrange that, I'm saying that off the record, of course. But her plan worked. The van's engine was running poorly, so they decided to steal another van, leaving the old one in its place. They stole a small church bus, with the name of the church on each side and the back. Nobody ever said these guys were smart. The switch was noticed less than thirty minutes later when the church called the local police. We were already in the area because of the farmer's wife and the gas station, so the local police called us. We asked for helicopter support, and they were apprehended during the time you were at the interrogation of the two female accomplices."

"So, it's all over? Other than identifying my attackers and getting Ashley home"

"Well, this is where your feisty wife comes into the picture. She heard these two guys talking about other girls they've abducted, and now we know where they were headed because the two female suspects gave us that information. Your wife, with no suggestions from us, by the way, said, in her own words, 'This ain't over yet. We need to find those other girls.'"

"What? Has Ashley gone crazy? I don't believe it," Adam spit the words out forcefully. How could she even think such a thing after all they'd gone through. He was ready to put this nightmare behind them, and there she was wanting to go off playing the heroine.

"I also find it hard to believe," Jenkins said. "But the officers with your wife are telling me she is very serious. The officers want me to have you talk to your wife, and we will abide by your joint decision."

"Yes. I need to talk some sense into Ashley. She's been through enough."

Norman Jenkins made a phone call and said, "Yes, please put her on." He then handed the phone to Adam.

"Hi, hon," Ashley said when she came on. "Are you okay? Is your head still in one piece?"

The others chuckled. The volume was loud enough for everyone to hear most of the conversation.

"Yes, I'm fine. I heard that they did rough you up a little."

"No big deal. Maybe not even any scars to brag about."

Then Adam said, "What's this crap about wanting to do more? You've done enough. I'm proud of how you disabled their van, but that's enough heroics."

"Listen, Adam, we know these guys have delivered at least two other girls to this stable, as they call it. Can you imagine what those girls have had to endure? Maybe they've even been killed. My conscience won't allow me to just send these two guys to prison. Even if we know where the stable is, they may not have a solid case against all of them without more evidence. Julie is not able to do more than she already has. She is really shaken. But I can get inside, and we can also take down the people who run the stable, and hopefully save the girls who are captive there."

"But Ashley, they're going to expect you to...ahh...sleep with their clients."

"My face is beat up right now. Moe and Larry, I mean Henry and Larry, were arguing about my face. Henry said they were going to only get $1000 for me because I was beat up, instead of the $2500. They can't offer me to clients until my face heals. If necessary, I'll keep picking the scabs to keep them bleeding. This is important to me, Adam. I need to do this for those girls."

"But how will they get the cooperation of those goons to deliver you and not spill the beans? They could get you killed, just to save their asses."

"I'll let the man from the State Police explain that to you, Adam. I think the difference between maybe 10 years or life in prison might be the answer. For now, I just need you to say okay. I know you'll worry, Adam, but would you rather be haunted by the faces of those other girls these guys have abducted? I've seen their pictures, and they were sweet, innocent girls, just like Julie. I can't leave them there, knowing I could have helped them."

"I know how you are Ash, and I love you for being so stubborn. Putting it that way, I know you'd never forgive me if I said no."

"I might forgive you, but would we be able to forgive ourselves if we ignore them?"

"You're right. I'll say yes, but please be careful. I love you too much to lose you."

"I will. The organized crime guys have a plan for me to contact them if things start going wrong. And I love you too, big guy. That's stealing a line from Lois, so I hope it's okay with her." Lois smiled when she overheard that!

Mr. Jenkins filled in Adam on the deal they had offered the two suspects if they cooperated. They had to have these two make the delivery, or the stable operators would know something was wrong. Both of the men and the church van were wired for sound, and if the listening devices were disabled, there were multiple Indiana, Kentucky, and Federal officers located nearby to respond.

That's when Adam laid down his ground rules. "I know I told Ashley she could go ahead with this, but I'm going to add something else into the plan. If you refuse, I'm withdrawing my approval."

"What do you want added, Mr. Walters?" Jenkins asked.

"Me," Adam said.

"What exactly do you mean?"

"I'm going along as one of the abductors. If you think I can replace one of those two guys, that's one option. Otherwise, I will be a third guy, who plans to take over the operation. I think I can act as stupid as those guys act, and they can introduce me as a new partner with access to more girls at that college. What do you think?"

"In fact, I like it. You can be the guy carrying a gun, rather than the two suspects, and they will need to cooperate entirely, knowing you're there to watch them."

"So then, you agree?

"I'll pass it by my superiors, and let the Kentucky officials know about the change, but I think adding you into the equation makes this safer for your wife."

"That's my main concern. So, you agree?"

"I agree."

Chapter 8

THE MEETING

Ashley and Adam didn't look like they should be a couple. Adam was well over six-feet tall and had that 'backwoods' look about him. Ashley was probably 5-foot-2 barely over 100 pounds and looked like a pixie, and just as pretty as a pop star. She was often mistaken for a teenager, despite being in her mid-thirties. The tug crews knew they had better respect her authority because she could really tell off a deckhand who did something stupid, particularly if it was due to safety issues on the job. At those times, Adam just stood back, watched her explode, and had a big grin on his face. Adam just loved to watch his "little girl" take charge of those situations.

Steve saw the concern Adam had for his wife as they drove behind Mr. Jenkins down I-65 past Indianapolis, to Seymour, Indiana, where they were to meet the organized crime units from both the Indiana and Kentucky State Police. There was also an FBI Agent from the Louisville Field Office.

Norman Jenkins introduced Adam and Steve to the team, and then they opened the door to the next room. Ashley had been giving a detailed, recorded statement of her experiences to an FBI Agent and stenographer, and when the door opened, she saw Adam. Ashley ran to Adam and jumped into his arms. Their combined emotions had these tough law enforcement people nearly in tears.

"Mr. Walters, this is one amazing lady. Not only did she delay her captors and disable their car, but now she insists on finding these other girls. And now we understand that you have asked to help with apprehending the stable personnel," Agent Brubaker, the FBI representative, said to Adam.

Ashley looked at Agent Brubaker, and then at Adam. Her eyes widened. "What? No! Adam will not be involved."

Adam uncharacteristically looked at Ashley and said, "Oh yes I will, or we head home to Michigan right now."

"I thought you agreed?" Ashley said, heatedly.

"Yes, I agreed, and you can help, as long as I'm there to keep an eye on you."

Agent Brubaker spoke up, "Mrs. Walters, or may I call you Ashley, we think it will be a good idea for Adam to be with you, and here's why. We have interrogated your two captors, and we consider the one called Larry, to be a very loose cannon. Despite our offer to recommend reduced charges for cooperation, we don't think he can be trusted. He's also the one who struck you, and he just told us, 'She had it coming.' We want him out of the plan, and we're suggesting that your husband will take over the role of Larry, as one of your abductors. Henry, on the other hand, is cooperating fully, and even Henry suggested that Larry should not be part of the delivery. And besides, Larry has one very bruised face from you breaking his nose."

"Well, Henry is a pretty dim-bulb himself, but he did try to stop Larry from hitting Julie, and he was mad when Larry hit me. Although that was probably because the bruises cost him $1500 of the $2500, which he expected to get for me. And tell me, just what are you expecting Adam to do?"

"We will have Henry introduce Adam as Larry. But we are going to reverse roles, and Adam will tell the people at the stable that Henry was the one to have struck you. Adam, speaking as Larry, will tell the stable operators that from now on, he is going to operate alone, because Henry is too rough on the girls. He'll tell them he has more college girls lined up back in Hammond, and he wants to know how the other girls worked out, that they delivered."

"Won't they know that Adam looks different from Larry?"

"Henry said that Larry didn't go into the drop-off last time, so they haven't seen Larry for a while. Adam is just as big as Larry, and we're going to darken up his hair and beard to look more like Larry."

Ashley was not happy about the revised plan to

have Adam involved, but Adam said, "We can be back in Michigan before dark."

"We aren't going to show up in that church minibus, are we?" Ashley then asked the agent.

Brubaker answered, "My, no! That sure showed how stupid these guys were. If we pulled into that church with that bus, with church markings all over, they would know something is wrong. We found an old white panel van, similar to the one that you disabled, and they will never notice any difference from what was used on their last delivery. We even banged up the rear wheel wells and tore off the gas door."

"Great. I couldn't believe they were taking that church van, but I had whispered to Julie that I was glad they were so stupid because it would be easy to track us from that point. I think you stopped them in less than an hour after that."

"And your brake fluid trick really worked, Mrs. Walters. The Indiana Police said that van wouldn't even start when they found it."

"Where did you get that idea, Ash?" asked Adam.

"I was going to try whatever I could find in the back of that van. I'd have used orange juice if it was there."

"I'm glad it wasn't sugar. People think that works, but it isn't true. The brake fluid did a lot more damage, even more than the water," said Agent Brubaker. "But now, I want to bring in Henry, full name Henry Thomas. We need to get him talking to Adam, and I want all references to Adam to use the name Larry, full name Larry Winkleson. That way there will be no slips to use the wrong name in front of anyone at the church.

Adam asked, "Why is this trafficking operation based in a church? I thought I was mistaken when I first heard that."

"These traffickers choose places they think will cover their operation. In this case, we hope the church's minister is not aware of what is taking place, but it wouldn't be the first time that a trafficker became an ordained minister through the internet, to hide his other business. We've seen school gymnasiums and health clubs used as well, with the townsfolk unaware of what is happening, right under their nose."

The Indiana State Trooper brought Henry Thomas into the meeting. When he saw Adam, he showed real fear. "Hey man, I'm sorry for your woman's face. Trust me, I tried to keep Larry from hitting her, but he was still pissed off about his nose. Then the gas tank, well...."

"Just sit down and shut up, Henry," Adam said. "And from now on, call me Larry."

"Okay, but I'm sorry," Henry said.

As the meeting continued, outlining the plans for the delivery of Ashley, Henry spoke up again, "Hey, where's the other girl?"

Agent Brubaker said, "She's traumatized by the situation. She's been escorted home to her family in Fort Wayne."

"Well, this ain't gonna work then. They're expecting two girls. Larry called 'em and said we had two girls."

Agent Brubaker appeared to be in shock. It was looking like the plan was going to fall apart. But then the Kentucky State Police representative with 'Tillison' on his name tag, spoke up, "Can I offer a suggestion? We've been working these trafficking groups the last couple years, and we have an undercover officer who has worked the bars and clubs where some abductions were happening around Louisville. She is similar to Miss Ashley here, looking much younger than her age. She could fill in as the second girl if you want me to call her."

"I think we should at least call her. If she could join our meeting, it would be much appreciated."

"I know she was in our Louisville Detail's Office when I left, even though it's Sunday. She could probably be here in less than an hour."

"Let's call her, please," Brubaker said.

While Tillison went off to make the phone call, Henry shared details with Adam about what they had done on previous trips to this same drop-off point.

"Where are they keeping the girls. Do they stay in the church?" Adam asked.

"I think they just process them at the church and then move them. We saw some girls there who we delivered before, but the next time we came, they were gone."

Adam appeared upset, saying, "Agent Brubaker, I don't like the idea of Ashley being moved. If she disappears from this church, we could lose her."

"I understand your concern. We'll have the site

under close surveillance, and if we notice any women being moved, we'll close down the operation immediately."

"Are you real sure you can do that? This is my wife's life we're playing with here."

"I assure you that Ashley's safety will be our first priority."

Steve was struck by everything he had seen and heard. He had come face to face with the crime of human trafficking and could not believe how far this crime actually reached. In just a matter of days, he now knew human trafficking to be a serious problem worldwide often overlooked by the average American who thinks it's just a 'Third-World' problem. He also was now aware that many teen runaways are eventually snatched by traffickers, some even lured through social media. Trevor had mentioned something about the demand for a 'better class of girls' recently leading to the kidnapping of young college students who were living away from home and probably wouldn't be quickly missed. One of the officers had also mentioned something about some being lured into fake modeling contracts to make money, leading to nude photos, porn, and finally sex trafficking.

It all weighed heavily on his mind when Steve excused himself and went outside to call Curt. "Dad, this is getting really scary. Ashley and Adam are going to make the trip to this delivery place. Now they're trying to find another female undercover officer to take the place of Julie."

"I think I'm going to head down there to be with you, Steve. I'll rent another car and head south. You just keep in touch and tell me where I should meet you."

"Thanks, Dad. This story is getting crazier by the minute."

"I'll catch up with you tonight, son. See you soon."

"Okay. I'd better get back into the meeting."

Almost an hour later, while the group was still talking, a young woman was ushered into the room. She appeared to be no more than seventeen. Officer Tillison stood up when she walked in. "You made great time Liz," he said, welcoming her and then introducing her to the group. "Everyone, please meet Officer Elizabeth Trent. She works with our Louisville sex-offenders detail."

Everyone stared at Officer Trent, finding it hard to believe that she was not a teenager.

"I know. I get that look a lot," she said. "I'm actually twenty-seven and a graduate of Eastern Kentucky University. I like law enforcement and I'm good at my job. My goal is to still get carded when I'm forty."

Everyone smiled and laughed a little.

Steve, however, continued to stare. She was the cutest girl he thought he'd ever seen. Officer Trent noticed him staring before he could look away.

"But you, young man. I'd like to get to know you better after this job is over." Steve turned red and was about to apologize when Liz added, "I did appreciate the extra attention, and I love a man who can blush."

Steve just dropped his stare to the table, and Liz smiled.

"So, tell me what's going on. Tillison said you might need my help. What can I do?" Officer Trent asked.

Agent Brubaker gave a rundown of the abduction, how Ashley had agreed to help secure the evidence needed for prosecution, and the desire to find and free the previously abducted young women. "Henry here is one of the abductors, and he has agreed to cooperate to possibly reduce his charges. The second abductor, Larry, is not cooperative, so this gentleman, Ashley's husband, who we are addressing as Larry, will be taking Larry's place for the delivery and pay-off. Henry tells us the drop point is expecting two girls, and the other abductee was very traumatized, so we had to send her home. Therefore, if you are willing, we're asking you to accompany Mrs. Walters as the second young lady in this delivery."

"Wow, Mrs. Walters, I can't believe you're willing to do this. You appear to be my age, so why don't you just want to go home with your husband?"

"Thank you, but we must share some similar genetics because I'm ten years older than you. I'm a tugboat captain, and I was grabbed by these two goons when they abducted the other girl. I heard them talking about other girls they've kidnapped like this, and I'm pissed off. I want to find those other girls and I hope we can nail a bunch of these guys."

Henry scowled and bowed his head at being called a goon, but nobody in the room even noticed.

"I like this lady. I'm in! I want to work with her. When is the delivery scheduled?"

"The delivery is to a church, and today is Sunday, so they'll head down tomorrow morning," Brubaker said.

"Is this that church in Little Spring? We've been suspecting that the minister has been involved for a while. We've seen him going into Gentlemen's Clubs in the area and disappearing in the back room. We figured he wasn't just looking to save those girls' souls."

"He wouldn't recognize you, would he?" Tillison asked.

"No. I spotted him, but he walked straight to the back, and never looked my way."

Even Henry was surprised by this and said, "You mean that tough-talking son of a bitch is a minister? Well damn!"

"Can we shorten up the group a little?" Officer Liz asked. "I'd like to talk with Ashley, and the man to be called Larry, with less of an audience. Maybe just one man from each agency: FBI, Kentucky, and Indiana would be enough."

As everyone rose to leave, Liz slid over to Steve and whispered, "Sorry if I embarrassed you, but that big blush sure was cute." Steve blushed again, and Liz smiled.

Chapter 9

ELIZABETH "LIZ" TRENT

Officer Elizabeth Trent, Liz for short, had been with the State Police for five years and gained a great reputation as an intelligent officer who was good at what she did. She hated sex offenders and traffickers in particular. Despite her superiors' concern for her safety, she often volunteered for undercover operations, posing as a potential victim, due to her appearance. Her fellow officers all believed she was only a teenager until they learned about her real age and accomplishments.

She had applied to the Kentucky State Police after college, thinking she would enter training to become a State Trooper, but when management saw her diminutive size, 5-foot-two, and youthful appearance, they felt she would not work out as a Trooper. However, they were impressed by her academic achievements, and particularly by her experience with the

University's Special Victim's Unit. She received all of the normal training for a State Trooper but also trained with the FBI's Human Trafficking and On-line Predator's Unit. The men in Liz's self-defense classes said they'd never want to be in a real fight with her because she fought 'dirty.' She could really take care of herself!

After Henry was ushered from the meeting room, along with the other agents and State Police officers, Officer Trent gave Ashley a warm hug. "Are you sure you want to do this? I could go in alone. Maybe say you escaped. It's my job after all."

Ashley was having a hard time thinking of Liz as a policewoman despite her experience and credentials. But of course, most people couldn't believe she was a tugboat captain. "They're expecting two of us, Officer Trent," Ashley answered, "and they know that one of us has a messed-up face.

"I heard so much about these people that run the stable, while in the van with these two guys, I don't want there to be any chance that they get away. And I want these two girls from Hammond to be found, if not a lot more. Seeing I have all the first-hand knowl-edge about what happened with Larry and Henry, I also want to be there when Henry makes his deal, to be sure he doesn't somehow clue them in that you're a cop. Sorry! I mean no disrespect. Larry was the worst of the two, but I certainly don't trust Henry. Both of these guys are scum, and Henry is only cooperating to help lighten his sentence."

"That's exactly what I wanted to warn you about. And what about this guy here, your husband? How did you talk him into this? No disrespect taken. I even call us cops. And call me Liz. Officer Trent is way too formal."

"Just the opposite, Liz," Ashley answered. "Adam refused to let me do this unless he came along. I'm going to make him suffer when we get back to work. On the tugs, I'm his boss. Understand?"

"Don't punish him too much though. Because with him posing as Larry, this will be a much safer operation. As much as we don't trust Henry, having Larry along would not have been good. I also understand Larry was the one who slugged you?"

"Any chance I could get five minutes alone with that guy before this is over?" Adam said.

"Officially, no! But crazier things have happened. I understand that Ashley already broke his nose. Ever thought about going into police work, Ashley?"

"Don't even tempt her," Adam said. "I'm afraid she'd say yes."

"By the way, and entirely off the subject, who's the cute young guy that was in the meeting? He had the nicest blush when I caught him eying me up."

"That's Steve Steiner," said Adam. "He's Curt Steiner's son. Curt is our boss. Steve was riding the tug with us when all this happened. He's the one who originally called the police up in Indiana Harbor."

"So, you two were on a tugboat and somehow got kidnapped by these guys?"

"Yup. Wrong place at the right time," Ashley said. "Just went to pick up some pizzas for the crew, and the other girl, Julie, was being set up by her roommates for Larry & Henry to snatch. But Julie's boyfriend had offered us a ride back to the tug, and then we found ourselves in the middle of it. In a way, it was lucky for Julie that we were involved, because she wouldn't have messed with them, and she'd be at that church by now. And that reminds me, Adam, what happened with Bill? Is he okay?"

"Curt checked up on him at the hospital and then went to visit Bill's grandmother. Bill has a fractured skull, but he'll recover. They sent him to a Chicago hospital, so some specialist could be with him during recovery."

"Which one of the guys did that, I assume it was Larry?" asked Liz.

"For sure," Adam said. "Larry pistol-whipped poor Bill when he tried to get them to let Julie loose. Larry's one brutal son of a bitch! Sorry."

"Well, I'm glad you're our new Larry then. But don't get involved with any of these guys unless things come apart. Watch my lead, and don't over-react. Once we witness Henry taking the payment, I have a small transmitter to signal the surveillance teams. If possible, I want Ashley and myself to continue to appear as the victims, and not let any of the perps see that we're in on the sting. Our teams will arrest everyone in that church, including Henry, and yes, also your hubby here. Adam, acting as Larry, will be in custody for a while, to keep Henry quiet, and to witness anything said by the others in custody. It's turning out that Adam will be a great inside witness, and you'll be the star witness at their trial. Are you okay with that?"

"If it helps to put these guys away, then I'm all for it."

"Once we have all the evidence we need, Adam will disappear, and the real Larry will take his place. Do you have any further questions, or should we get this show on the road?"

"I'm as ready as I can be," said Ashley.

"I'm ready but worried," said Adam.

"It's okay to be nervous and even to look that way, Adam. The low-life, victim-runners at this level of trafficking look confident around their victims, but when they meet those in charge of these operations, they tend to appear pretty cowardly, because they no longer can use brute force to be in charge."

"That's good, because I may be looking pretty scared."

"Now Ashley, I have a bit of bad news for you. Seeing we're not making the delivery until tomorrow, you need to go one more night without a shower or a change of clothes. Wash up a little tonight but keep that wonderful body odor. They are not expecting someone smelling like soap, and I'm sure Henry and Larry did not offer."

"I sorta' expected that. So, Adam will have to stay away from me for another night, I guess."

"I might suffer through it, Ash. Watch out," Adam said.

Liz gave both of them a big smile. "I like you guys!"

Liz called everyone back into the room and said they were ready to move over to Kentucky, where they would spend Sunday night. After a tension-filled night spent in a small motel, far from the drop-off church location, Officer Trent, Ashley, and Adam came out of their rooms. Ashley was looking miserable with her three-day-old clothes and dirty, bruised face.

The new, beat-up van was brought around, and Liz tested the small transmitter.

Curt had arrived the night before, and he asked, "I know that Steve and I aren't part of this operation, but we are concerned about Ashley's and Adam's welfare. Where can we wait, close enough to that church, but not be a problem for you?"

"Agent Brubaker, do you have an office near Little Spring where the Steiners can be comfortable?" Liz asked.

"Well, Fort Knox is only twenty minutes away, and they have a nice visitor's center there. We can set up a room for Curt and Steve, and we can keep them updated on the operation. How does that sound?"

"I think that's great," said Liz. "Okay with you two?" she asked, looking directly at Steve.

Steve saw an obvious twinkle in Liz's eyes, and he thought she was now flirting with him. He didn't mind, except that now he felt very self-conscious about her being six years older than him.

Curt said, "We really want to be around when this is all over. You understand?"

"Sure," Liz replied, "but you may not understand as yet, our Larry-impersonator will be in custody along with Henry here. Our Larry-impersonator will guarantee that Henry plays his part correctly. You understand that, don't you, Henry? One wrong word or action from you, and we will not tell the judge that you cooperated."

"Yes, Ma'am," Henry said. "I understand."

Officer Trent had changed clothes, and she looked totally disheveled. Her hair was wet and knotted, and she had on those old, smelly clothes. Her face had smudges like she had been wiping away tears.

"So, Ashley, do I look the part?" she asked.

"If it wasn't for a different face, I'd swear that you were Julie."

"And how about the body odor? Bad enough? I keep these sweaty old clothes in a sealed bag, just for occasions like this."

"Yes. Suitably terrible," Ashley said. "Now I understand why Agent Brubaker didn't want me to shower or wash up yesterday, even though I begged for a shower. He wanted me to smell as bad as you," Ashley said, smiling.

"Right, Ashley. They'll expect us to look and smell pretty bad. I'd been meaning to tell you how bad you smell, by the way!" Liz said with a chuckle.

Ashley was thinking that Liz was doing very well to keep a light attitude for what, even to her, must have been a tense morning. As much as Ashley wanted to do this, she did have to admit to herself that she was getting scared, as the actual operation was about to begin. Now that Adam was also involved, she was even more afraid.

After the State Police and FBI left, to be in their position close to the Little Spring church location, the four of them piled into the van. Adam was driving, and Henry was in the passenger seat. Ashley and Liz sat on the floor in the back. Liz could tell that Ashley was looking less confident than when they were just talking about the operation, so she reached out and took Ashley's hand, giving her a comforting squeeze.

"Funny," Ashley said. "On the drive down, I was the one to comfort Julie, but now you're comforting me."

"Yes, the real thing, when it finally stares you in the face, is very disquieting. It's a good thing to look scared. You're supposed to be scared. And I have another request, for the sake of realism. When we pull into the church parking lot, I'll tell you when, but we are both going to wet ourselves."

"Really? That seems a little much," Ashley said.

"When the time comes, it may just feel natural. Trust me. Nerves actually work that way. What do you think young Julie would have done as she arrived here? And a side effect, the last thing on these guys' minds will be sex with a smelly, dirty girl, who just peed herself. I don't think they would even think about that, but just to be safe, the worse we look and smell at this point, the better off we are."

"Wow, Liz! How did you learn all these things? You look so young and innocent."

"Remember, I've been doing this for five years, and even before that, I remember the first time I saw a rape victim while working at the UK Police Department. She told the investigator that during the rape, she vomited in the guy's bed. He stopped immediately and drove the girl out to a country road, where he slugged her and left her. She told us that the last thing she did was to pee and defecate in the guy's back seat. When they located the guy, he was still trying to clean the mess out of his car."

"Oh my. This is real-world stuff. Not what we average citizens ever think about."

"I've never had to go beyond the peeing stage, but it's good to know what else turns off a perp."

Just then, Henry spoke up, "The church is right ahead. What do you want me to do?"

"You and Larry go into the church as you had planned. Stay at the door, so you can keep an eye on us in the van. I assume the minister is your contact. Tell him you have two for delivery and ask him where to take us. Ask him if he has the cash ready for you."

As Henry and Adam got out of the van, Liz said, "It's show time Ashley. I hope your bladder is full."

Chapter 10

THE DELIVERY

Henry knocked on the church's basement door and pushed a button next to it. They heard a buzzer deep inside the church, and a minute later they heard footsteps before the door opened.

Henry said, "We have that delivery from Hammond. Where do you want them?"

"We expected you yesterday. Where've you been?" a gruff-looking man dressed in tattered jeans and an old, sweaty T-shirt, said, answering the door.

Adam stared him in his eyes. "We had trouble with one of them. Had to get a new van."

"You got our cash ready?" Henry asked.

"Need to inspect the merchandise first. Drive to the side door over there. Keep close to the door so nobody sees them coming in."

The two men got back into the van and drove to the side door, then opened the back door to get the women out. Adam took Ashley's arm, and Henry took Officer Trent's arm and led them to the door. The door opened immediately and then shut quickly after all four had entered. The men in the church led them into a back room in the church basement and turned on the lights.

An older man with long hair tied in a ponytail was the first to speak. "This one is damaged goods," he said, looking at Ashley's face.

"As I said, one of them caused trouble, and she got slugged," Adam said.

"You realize she's unusable until that heals. We won't pay for damaged goods."

"Wait a minute. We were told it just reduced the pay by $1000, not no pay," Henry said.

"I think we told you we'd only pay up to $1000. This one's pretty banged up, so what if she doesn't heal properly. We'll give you $500 for her. The other one's okay, so you get the $2500 promised."

Henry started to grumble, but Adam spoke up, "We'll take the $3000. I'll take the rest out of Henry's hide when we get home. So, how are those other girls doing? The ones we dropped here before?"

"That's none of your business now, is it?"

"Well, I thought we might sample the goods before we head back. Give you some of your money back."

"In that case, just stop at the Gentlemen's Club out near the Highway at Radcliffe. Tell the guy at the door that the minister sent you. He'll set you up in the back room."

"Okay then. We'll settle on the $3000, and we'll be on our way," Henry said,

The second man returned through a back door of the room and handed Henry a paper bag. As Henry opened the bag, the man said, "There's six packs of twenty's, twenty-five in each pack."

Just then, Liz fell to the floor and started moaning. "Holy shit, guys. When did you feed these girls last? And damn, they smell awful, like they pissed themselves."

"After they messed up our old van, we had to make up time," Adam said. "We didn't stop at all today."

As Liz started to move, Ashley saw her push the side of her shoe. The minister led Henry and Adam to the side door, where they had entered, and Adam said, "Hey, can I use a restroom? Like I said, we haven't stopped all day. With that smell in the van, I really need to go bad."

"Show him the toilet down the hall, Greg," The minister said.
"What about you, Henry? You must be ready to pop as well. We don't want to get to that Gentleman's Club and head right into the John, do we?"

"I s'pose you're right," Henry said, and he followed behind Adam and the guy called Greg.

Adam took as much time as possible in the toilet, then came out with Henry, and they went back to the minister where Adam asked him if he wanted "more of these," these being girls.

"Undamaged, of course," Adam added. "We have our eye on a couple more at that Hammond college."

"I think that four from one school is enough. You'd better try another school, so nobody gets suspicious. Remember not to get girls who live with their families near the school. If they're alone in an apartment is best. Then nobody misses them for a while."

Adam extended his hand for a handshake, but the minister pulled away. Adam thought it was crazy that this minister thought he was above the transporters. He was the one profiting from trafficking these women. Adam pulled his hand back and opened the door. There were about twelve men outside, all with guns drawn, including the FBI Agents and the Kentucky State Troopers. In the background were the three Indiana State Police, but with no guns drawn.

"Holy shit," yelled Adam. "What's going on?"

"You're under arrest," said Agent Brubaker.

"I'm so glad you're here, officer," the minister said. "These two men came in here demanding money from our weekend offerings. We just gave them what we had, and they said they were going to leave these two homeless women here. We're so relieved that you must have been looking for them. Thank the Lord!"

Brubaker looked at the minister and frowned. "Tillison, have your men search the entire building. Arrest anyone they find, including these two."

"What do you mean, officer? I'm the pastor of this church, Reverend Albert Willis. I'm a man of God and these men are the criminals."

"We've been watching this trafficking operation for

the last six months. We know who you really are, Mr. Willis. I won't use Reverend with you because I don't believe you deserve that title."

The Kentucky Troopers led Henry, Adam, Albert Willis, and Greg out in handcuffs. The Troopers then came downstairs with an older man and woman, whom they had found in the church office. They looked like they were ready to faint. "We found these two upstairs, Agent Brubaker. The office safe was open, and it is piled with stacks of twenties. There has to be over $25,000 in the safe."

"Go back up there and count it. Be sure to have one man from each agency as a witness, and we will confiscate the money until we've determined the source. If it was collected as church offerings, we'll return all or a portion that is church property."

Agent Brubaker then addressed the old couple, who were looking stunned, "And who are you, and what were you doing in the office?"

The man spoke, "We are Emily and Edmund Donaldson. We work as the church staff. Emily keeps the records and I perform maintenance. May I ask what's going on? Why have you arrested Reverend Willis?"

"We'll get to that in due time. My name is Leonard Brubaker, Agent with the Louisville Field Office of the FBI. If Emily is the church record keeper, I think she will need to show us the church records for donations, so we can determine how much of that cash belongs to the church."

"I don't even have the combination for that safe,"

said Emily. "I count the offerings on Monday morning, and I deposit the money into the church bank account on Monday afternoon. I've never seen that cash before. I always wondered what was in that safe."

"Are you telling me that you do not believe the cash in that safe is from church funds?"

"Certainly not that I am aware of," said Emily.

"Well, Mr. & Mrs. Donaldson, I'd like you to also witness the counting of that money, and if you're willing, please show our agents your records of church income, donations, bank statements, and so on. Would you be willing to do that?"

"We will certainly cooperate," Edmund Donaldson said.

"Good. Go back up there and count that money. Be sure to have one man from each agency as a witness, as well as the Donaldsons, and we will confiscate the money until we've determined the source," Brubaker continued. "If it was collected as church offerings, we'll return all or a portion that is church property."

"Am I to assume that Greg and our minister are in trouble?" Mr. Donaldson asked.

"Yes, he is in trouble, but for now, I cannot tell you anything more. We will ask you to come to the State Police Detachment and make a statement," Brubaker said to the elderly Donaldson.

Brubaker then took Tillison aside and told him to keep the Donaldsons busy until they could talk to Liz and see what would happen next.

Liz met the agents and officers, with the Donaldsons

who were on their way back to the church office. She was relieved the plan had worked.

"Not only did the hand-off and the pay-off go as planned, Brubaker, but Ashley's husband deserves a medal," Liz told Brubaker. "That guy got more information out of that minister than I ever could have. He admitted that they received several women from that Hammond campus, and he advised them to move to a different campus in the future. Then Adam asked how the previous girls were doing, and of course, the good reverend clammed up. So, Adam said they wanted to 'sample the goods', and the minister's greed kicked in. He told Adam to stop at the Gentleman's Club in Radcliffe and tell the guy at the front door that the minister sent them. We've been trying to do something like that for a few years, and Adam gets the key password in just a couple minutes.

"With Adam, our fake-Larry, being held with the others, I don't see how we can act on that information for a few days. By then, the word of the minister's arrest will have spread to them."

"I have an idea," Liz continued. "Get Ashley and me to a hotel, so we can clean up. I have my clean clothes in one of the Troopers' cars but have someone buy Ashley a nice outfit. Have a lady do the buying and tell her we need some makeup to cover Ashley's bruises. Ask Curt and Steve if they will act as our dates, and we'll all go to that Club. I see lots of couples go into those back rooms together. I guess that's a turn-on for some women, to see their partner get a lap-dance, or possibly more, from those girls in the back. If Ashley recognizes those girls from Hammond, based on the photos she's seen, that's great. But in any case, we should be able to see enough illegal action in the back to close that place down. We need to do this tonight, before the word leaks out on our bust, here at the church. Try to keep the Donaldsons busy all day, but I think if you ask them to keep this quiet until the news hits the networks, they'll probably cooperate. I think Mrs. Donaldson was pretty shocked to see all that money in that safe."

"Wow! You came up with all of that right now?" asked Agent Brubaker when Liz was done.

"As soon as Adam got that info from the minister, I knew that Adam couldn't go, so my mind started working on a solution. And hey, Ashley, I just realized that I never asked if you are okay with this additional plan?"

"Of course, Liz. It's a great idea. I hope we find the Hammond girls, but maybe there will be others there who are looking to escape. Speaking of escape, why don't these girls just run away? They can't be watching them constantly."

"At first, it's the trauma and fear of bodily harm, but then they sometimes drug the girls. Once they've been forced to have sex, they're ashamed, and they stay because they think that their life can never return to normal again. But if some of them appear to be the type to run, they threaten to harm their family if they run away. Although that may not happen, the girls have witnessed the brutality of these guys enough to believe that their family members could be harmed, or even killed.”

“I never knew that such terrible people existed outside of the movies.”

“Some of these perps are worse than what you see in the movies. There are a lot of people out there, both men and women, who feel they have nothing to lose. Just look at the two guys who nabbed you. Do you think their conscience is bothering them right now? Trust me, they are just trying to save their own ass.”

“I don’t understand why you like this job, Liz.”

“Look at it this way, Ashley. Every time I testify against one of these guys in court, and I hear the judge sentence them, I get the biggest high you can imagine, for the accomplishment I was part of producing. Just like you did, worrying these scumbags might get away with this abduction, you then wanted to follow through to see them pay for doing something terrible. I’ve just made a career of it, which will probably end as I start showing my age. For now, I use my talents to catch these bastards. Sorry! I try not to swear, but I got carried away.”

“I certainly understand, Liz. I guess it’s just the tension I felt today that was much worse than I expected. I knew that Larry and Henry had guns when they took us, so I worried that the minister or Gary may have had a gun too.”

“It’s usually the lower-level guys, like your transporters, who carry. The minister is already thinking up ways to avoid charges, and he knows that having a gun would make it very difficult to claim his innocence. In this case, I can't wait to see the look on his face when he finds out that Larry is your Adam. I'm hoping to be on the opposite side of the two-way mirror when that happens. And he won't find out that I'm a cop until his lawyer serves me with a subpoena for a deposition."

"Well, Liz. I respect you for what you do. Seeing you in action today, thinking on your feet, was very impressive."

"The only thing I did was to feign a faint and keep my mouth shut. Your Adam did all the work."

"I was proud of him today. He's normally so quiet that I wonder if he's fallen asleep while I'm talking. But today, he surprised me."

"Yes, you can be very proud of him. But for now, let's get to that hotel, get cleaned up, and head out on our date. We can hopefully make a few more arrests before we call it a day. Our two handsome men are awaiting us."

"I guess I don't quite understand what we are doing tonight. I mean going as couples. I thought only men went to these clubs."

"You'll be surprised by how many women will be there tonight, particularly in the back room. I guess some women get turned on seeing their men fool around with other women. It's a strange world, Ashley."

Ashley and Liz arrived at the hotel where two rooms

were ready for them. There were clean clothes and makeup laid out and ready for them. Liz said, "When you're dressed, come to my room with that makeup. I'll help you cover up your bruises."

Ashley stood under the hot shower longer than she remembered ever doing in her life. Three days without a shower after sweating in the back of that van, was not an experience she wanted to repeat. She thought of how casually Liz was handling things. The ease with which she had casually said it was time to wet themselves, just as casually as Ashley would tell her deckhands to toss a facing line to the guy on the barge. What an amazing woman. Ashley did notice that the trooper had spread some black garbage bags in the back seat for them to sit on, for the trip back to the hotel. They may have respected what she and Liz had done, but they didn't want to be reminded by the odor on their seats for many days to come.

The clothes some policewoman had purchased for her were classy, but a little large for her. Ashley figured the Gentleman's Club was not a place where people would be judging her fashion sense. She blow-dried her hair and took her makeup to Liz's room. Liz looked like a model, even though her clothes were just jeans and a stretch knit top. She certainly looked better than she had all day, and Ashley was afraid that poor Steve was going to stare and be embarrassed again. Ashley thought that maybe she should tell Liz that Steve was just about to turn twenty-one, but she decided it was best to say nothing. Steve was a great-looking guy, easily passing for mid-twenties, and Curt had raised him well. He respected women, but it was obviously difficult for Steve to ignore Liz's good looks. Her tight jeans and form-fitting top were going to be hard for Steve to overlook tonight.

Liz did a much better job of applying the makeup, but when she told Ashley to use the lipstick, Ashley said she never wore lipstick and seldom wore any makeup."

"I think the lipstick is necessary to look the part tonight. I agree that you don't need lipstick, and to-morrow, you can go back to natural. But tonight, I think both of us need to look a bit glitzy."

Ashley and Liz went down to the hotel lobby and met Agent Brubaker, who was instructing Curt and Steve on what was expected of them. Steve noticed Liz immediately. Liz said nothing but seemed to ap-preciate Steve's attention.

"When we get into the back room, the girls may want to give lap dances," Liz said, quickly switching to her professional self. "You can just tell them we like to watch for a while, but order drinks and give big tips, which will work for a while. Ashley and I are going to see if the girls from Hammond are there, but eventu-ally, we'll need to spread more money around, in order to stay in the back room. Have either of you ever been in the backroom of a Gentleman's Club before?"

"I've never seen the inside of a Gentleman's Club, no less the back room," Curt said. "I've heard sailors describe it, but that's not the same, I guess."

"What about you, Steve? Dare you admit it in front of your dad?" Liz asked, looking pointedly at Steve.

Steve was as red as he'd ever been. "Sorry. Me neither," he mumbled.

"Don't be sorry, Steve. That's worth bragging about to a woman these days. Congratulations to both of you for being nice guys."

Steve calmed down and Curt smiled at Liz, after seeing the pleased look on Steve's face. "So then, what do you want Steve and I to do?" Curt asked Liz.

"First of all, here's a roll of fives. Start stuffing them in the girl's G-strings. That's expected in the back, even though guys use singles out front. Then, Curt, I'm going to have you do this when I give you the signal. Tell the pushiest girl of the bunch that you want her to give me a grind. Say it this way, 'Give my son's girlfriend a grind. That turns us on.' I'll be waiting for them to invite us into the private rooms, and if I hear the right terms, I'll pull my badge. I'm just hoping Ashley sees a familiar face by then, and I'll push my transmitter to call in our troops. And remember, when we get inside the front door, tell the host, 'The minister sent us'."

Curt and Steve were looking at one another, thinking, *just what have we gotten into here?*

A few minutes later, Liz directed Curt to the Club, just a couple of miles from the hotel. The State Patrol officers were already in position.

"Can I help you?" asked the host who greeted them at the reception booth.

Curt was shaky, but he managed to say, "The minister sent us."

"Ahh, yes. Just head back to Trudy, by the back door," and he gave the woman a hand signal.

Trudy opened the back door and said, "I like to see couples getting it on together. Enjoy yourselves."

Ashley took in the atmosphere as they walked through the club. She had heard about these Gentlemen's Clubs but seeing one first-hand was eye-opening. She expected more nudity and was surprised to see the two girls dancing on the stage were bare-chested, but still had on a G-string. She figured it might come off eventually. The surprising thing was the number of waitresses serving drinks, and the number of glasses she saw on the tables. Not only were the customers tipping the dancers, but the waitresses were being tipped very well.

The back room was quieter than out front, and the girl dancers were right there, next to the customers. Most tables were just a single man, and as Liz predicted, there were two tables with couples, other than themselves. These girls were scantily clad, but not topless. Then she saw a man and one of the dancers come out of a private enclosure, with curtains across the entrance. The dancer was adjusting her clothing in a way that Ashley suspected was where the serious stuff was happening.

Once they were seated, they were offered drinks and both guys asked for a beer. Liz ordered a vodka tonic for her and Ashley. Then the four of them sat, holding their drinks, but not drinking them when the drinks arrived. The girls started coming to them almost immediately. Curt told them they just wanted to watch for a while, and politely handed the woman a five.

"Stuff it in her drawers, Curt," Liz said with a huge smile on her face.

"See the girl behind the bar? That's one of the Hammond girls," Ashley whispered to Liz.

Liz turned to Steve and asked him to ask for the girl behind the bar if any of the other girls came by to ask if they needed anything. Let's see what she says."

It didn't take long, and a young girl came up, asking Steve if he'd like a lap dance. Steve was better prepared than Curt had been and said, "I'd really like that girl making drinks behind the bar. Can you send her over?" as Steve nicely shoved a five into the girl's waistband.

"She's been a bad girl lately, so she's stuck behind the bar tonight."

"Well then, can I just go talk to her? I like her looks."

"I'll ask the manager and let you know," the girl said, with a worried look on her face.

The girl walked away and was seen talking with an older woman the group hadn't noticed before. She was sitting in the corner of the room. The older woman went to the bar and had a serious conversation with the girl mixing drinks while pointing at their table. The girl nodded and walked toward them.

Liz asked her to take a seat next to Steve.

"Don't show any reaction to this," Ashley said to her, "but is your name Britta Spencer? You're a student at Purdue-Hammond?" Tears began to well up in the girl's eyes.

"Do you want to get out of here?" Liz asked her.

Britta said, "They'll hurt my mom if I leave."

"Not if they're in jail, sweety," Liz said. "I have an army of Troopers ready to arrest everyone you tell me to."

"Can we get my friends out of here too?" she asked.

"You bet, honey. We hold everyone in the place, then you and your friends get to tell us who to arrest, and who we let go home."

"Then yes, I want out of here," Britta said.

"Steve, you keep pushing those fives at Britta, while I push this transmitter."

In less than three minutes, the Troopers had secured every door, and Britta and three of her friends were holding court. As each person walked by them, they pointed out the staff, dancers who had been working there a long time, those who had threatened them, and those who were just customers. In a few instances, they'd say, "What about this guy? He's a customer but he hurt me?"

"Let's hold him on perversion," one of the State Police investigators said.

"Good idea," said Liz.

Then Britta said, "What about this guy. He works here, but he's always been nice to us, and he sneaks us extra food when he can."

Liz said, "Take this guy's name and number. Let's see if we can find him a better job." And Britta smiled.

It took over two hours to sort through the people in the club. Twelve people were arrested, three held on perversion, and the names and addresses of all the customers were recorded and told to stop frequenting such establishments. If they showed up in another raid, they might be charged. The dancers who were over eighteen had not broken any laws and were let go, with advice to go back to school. There wasn't anything the authorities could do to help them, as they hadn't broken the law, although the Club was charged because the under-aged girls were serving alcohol.

Britta, and her three friends, felt freedom for the first time in months. All four had been threatened with possible injury to their family, and Liz told them they could extend their captors' sentences if they would agree to file charges against those who threatened them. Three of the girls agreed, including both of the girls who had been abducted by Larry & Henry. Those two women seemed to relish the possibility of seeing Larry's and Henry's sentences extended.

"What about Trisha and Darlene?" Britta asked. "They're the ones who set us up."

"They're already in custody. Believe it or not, it was our Uber driver in East Chicago who located them for the police," Ashley told Britta. "We need to introduce you to Trevor Jordan when we get back to Hammond. That guy is responsible for saving each one of us because he took responsibility for some strangers whom he had only just met. I'll tell you more about that later," Ashley added.

"Ladies, I think we've done our job here tonight. I'll have this nice Trooper escort you to our hotel and get you a couple of rooms. You wouldn't mind sharing, two to each room? Do you have any belongings we need to get?" Liz asked.

"Oh, yes. We need to have you arrest our house mother. She's more like our prison warden. The four of us have been held at her house because we weren't cooperative. Can we go there to get our things? I'd love to see you cuff her. Mrs. Donaldson is a real bitch," Britta said.

Brubaker, Liz, and Ashley looked at each other. How had they not seen that? It all made sense now, the question of why Greg had not worried about leaving that church safe open with the Donaldsons in the office. He knew they could be trusted because they were part of the team. They sure had put on a great act. Luckily, the State investigators had kept them busy long enough that they never had a chance to warn the club's manager.

Brubaker immediately stepped away to make a phone call. He came back a few seconds later. "They were just about to leave," he said, grinning. "I told the guys to arrest them. Young ladies, can we ask you to stop by our Field Office before you go to retrieve your belongings? We have someone we'd like you to identify."

Curt and Steve had been waiting patiently behind

the girls holding court. Curt had called his wife, Lois, who was still in the hotel back in Hammond and tried to explain that he and Steve were in a Gentleman's Club. For the first time in years, Lois seemed to be speechless. When Curt told Lois he was Ashley Walters' date for the evening, and Steve had a date with an undercover policeman, Lois said, "I assume this is all some sort of practical joke?"

"Oh, and did I tell you that Adam Walters is in jail?" Curt continued.

"Okay. That's enough. Call me tomorrow when you sober up."

"Don't you want to talk to Steve?" Curt asked.

"No, you've just coached him to back up your silly story. Good night, and I love you, despite your twisted sense of humor."

"Love you too, Babe."

"She didn't believe a word of it, did she?" Steve said after Curt hung up the phone.

"Not a word," and Curt started laughing.

Liz looked on in confusion. "What's your dad laughing about?" she asked Steve.

"He just tried to explain this evening to my mom."

"She didn't believe any of it, did she?"

"Nope."

"Maybe I can meet your mom at the trials. You realize, Steve, you're also a witness now. You did a great job tonight, by the way. Getting Britta over to our table like you did, made things happen much quicker. Thank you for thinking on your feet."

"I kinda got into it. I'm glad my dad didn't need to try that grinding and private room idea. He's devoted to my mom, and he would have had a tough time doing that."

"Both you and your dad are great guys. I can see that. Maybe I need to move up to Michigan. I wouldn't mind seeing more of your family."

Steve felt the sweat on his forehead and started to blush again.

Later that evening, Brubaker took the four young women to confront the Donaldsons, and as much as Liz wanted to see their reaction, she felt that Ashley had had a long, stressful day and needed to get a good night's sleep. So, Liz instead called her supervisor and told him she needed three additional rooms at the hotel, two for the women hostages they had freed, and one for Curt and Steve Steiner, until they had their statements recorded the following day.

Liz then turned to Curt. "Would you mind chauffeuring this weary group back to our hotel? I've arranged a room for you guys, until after we get your statements tomorrow. Then I think you'd better retrieve Mrs. Steiner from her hotel in Hammond before she starts to wonder about you guys. If necessary, I can come to meet her sometime, maybe up in Michigan. I can better explain the reason you were in a Gentleman's Club. I'll meet you in the lobby for breakfast at eight o'clock."

Curt agreed to drive the group back to the hotel where Liz and Ashley walked toward the elevator toward their rooms and Curt and Steve stayed behind to chat.

The following morning, Liz was the first to arrive in the breakfast room. She soon realized that the breakfast buffet, or 'free breakfast' as they called it, left a lot to be desired. So, she Googled the area for restaurants and found a locally owned diner with a 5-star rating. Slowly, the rest of the State Police investigators, FBI Agents, Curt and Steve, and finally Asley and Adam appeared. Adam had been released from his faked arrest late during the previous night and was dropped off at the hotel for a reunion with Ashley.

"Where are the four girls?" Liz asked.

Ashley looked worried. "Three of them are on their way down, but you remember the girl who wasn't willing to press charges? Well, she's disappeared. I'll let the other three girls explain what happened."

The three young girls finally came into the buffet. The two from Hammond had stayed together, and the other two girls had shared a room. "You are Roberta, right? asked Liz. "What happened to

Leslie?"

"We both called our family last night, like you suggested," Roberta said to Liz. "My mom was so happy to hear from me. Thank you for letting us use that cell phone. I called first and then Leslie called her brother. Leslie's mom is dead, and her dad disappeared when she was young, so she and her brother were on their own. I didn't realize that Leslie also has a younger sister, who just turned fifteen. Her sister disappeared about two months ago, and the brother suspects she may have been dating a local guy. When Leslie heard the name, I heard her scream, 'No, not him! That's who took me away.'"

"So, Leslie left the hotel?" asked Liz.

"I didn't know that she had. That was around two o'clock, and I consoled her and said we'd ask for your help this morning. I fell asleep and when I woke up this morning, she was gone."

"Did she take that cell phone with her?'

"Yes, she did. I'm sorry."

"No, it may be a good thing. All of our phones have a tracking app on them, so as long as she has the phone with her, we can find her. Do you know where Leslie's brother and sister live?"

"I heard her mention Independence, over near Cincinnati. At least that's where her brother lives. He works on the riverboats."

"Do you have any idea what her plans were?" Liz asked.

"Not really. I just heard her tell her brother, 'I'll find her, and then I'll kill that bastard.' She seemed mad enough that she might just do it. That's when I told her we would get your help this morning."

"You could have called me in the middle of the night, but don't worry. I'm sure we can find her. I assume she had no money?"

"Maybe ten bucks at most. The Club didn't let us keep our tips, but once in a while, we could hide some when they weren't looking."

"Officer Tillison, could you get this out on the radio right away?" Liz asked. "She's probably looking for rides on I-64. That's the fastest route to Independence. And ask your contacts with the truckers to spread the word as well. They're good at watching for runaways but tell them this is a special case. Ask them to call us if they suspect they've seen her. We don't want to scare her into running. Here's the number of the phone she has, so, try the tracking app as well."

"I'll get the boys right on it, Liz," Officer Tillison replied, taking the number and walking away.

Liz then explained that she wanted to go to a better restaurant located just outside of town. While they waited for Tillison to make the call, Liz called the restaurant and asked if they had a private room to seat twelve for breakfast. The woman on the other line told Liz that they would open their Rotary and Kiwanis room, which wasn't being used that morning.

"We'll head to the restaurant," Liz said when she got off the phone. "I think it's called the Backstreet or something, where we can have some privacy to talk. We need to get the statements from all these great people, and then we'll arrange transportation to get them home." Tillison joined them and signaled to Liz that word had gone out. She nodded and continued, "I don't want to delay them any more than necessary. And I think I got Curt and Steve in trouble with Mrs. Steiner, so, I may need to take some leave soon, so I can go meet her." Liz gave Steve a little grin, which started Steve blushing again.

On the way to breakfast, Liz got a call from Tillison, "She didn't get far. A trucker spotted her at a truck stop on I-64. She was asking for someone to buy her breakfast and he offered. That's also where the tracking app shows that phone. I have a Trooper on the way and told him to treat her with kid gloves. He'd heard about the bust last night, so he'll be kind with her and offer to help with her sister."

"Wonderful. Be sure to give me that Trooper's name later, so I can thank him."

"He's perfect for this situation. I know him, and he has teenage kids at home, so he understands."

"Couldn't have worked out better. We'll meet her at the Louisville Detachment office. Thanks loads, Tillison."

Liz told everyone the good news when they arrived at the breakfast diner. She told the three remaining girls, plus Ashley, Adam, Curt and Steve, that she had arranged for several investigators to take their statements, in order to speed things along. Seeing the other three girls were from Indiana, there would be three Indiana State cars meeting them in Louisville, to drive them home.

Breakfast was surprisingly silent. Everyone was deep in thought, due to the unnerving experiences they all had over the last several days, or months for the three girls. Adam was constantly smoothing Ashley's hair, and she smiled at him, knowing how afraid he had been about her safety. The three girls were deep in thought, and Liz knew from previous experiences, that these girls would need a lot of counseling before they could return to a normal life, though it would never be the same. Ashley and Adam would be fine, because they had each other, and they both understood what the other had gone through. But they'd be very careful around strangers for a long time. Curt seemed to be fine, and surprisingly, so was Steve. He sure seemed to be much more mature than most guys his age. Great parenting, Liz suspected, and the responsibilities he learned from working the tugboats with his father.

Liz knew that her attraction to Steve would look weird, maybe even somewhat suspect to others. She never tried to judge a person by their age, and at first, she thought that Steve looked to be in his mid-20s. Her initial teasing was just to get a rise out of him, which it did. But most cocky guys would have started flirting with her in response, but Steve didn't do that. His blushing was the thing that then attracted her. Most guys don't blush like that. The second thing which caught Liz's attention was how quickly Steve caught on to the serious issues at hand and reacted without needing a lot of instructions. Liz could see that his father, Curt, had the same traits, so Steve's parents were very responsible for Steve's serious side. Young or not, Liz wanted to see more of Steve Steiner, but that might require some explanation to Mr. and Mrs. Steiner. Liz was sure they would be concerned about their son being *stalked* by an older woman. She didn't feel that their age difference was that great, particularly because their personalities seemed to mesh well. But others' perceptions would be different.

After breakfast, the string of cars proceeded to the State Police Post, detachment office, where the two girls from Hammond identified Henry and Larry as their abductors. "Can I go inside and spit in their faces," one of the girls asked.

"I'd rather you don't see them until their trial," Liz replied. "But I certainly understand, and judges who handle cases like this are usually willing to let you give them a full tongue lashing, even overruling their lawyer's objections."

Liz asked one of the girls abducted in Hammond why her family had never reported her missing. The girl replied, "I guess that's my fault. I'm the middle child of five, and I was always the rebel. Not that my parents don't love me, but when I moved away to college, we had a bit of a falling-out and I told my mom that college was my time, and she should just leave me alone. Then I decided to stay for summer classes and needed a new place to stay. When Trisha and Darlene offered me a bedroom for $100 a month, I took it. I told my mom I'd see her at Thanksgiving, and for her to just stay out of my life. She did!"

"So, what will you do now?" Liz asked.

"I'm going home, giving my mom a big hug, and telling her what a jerk I've been. These last months were terrible, but they didn't destroy me. I've learned to keep the people who love me as close to me as possible. I'll go back to school, but maybe next year.

Right now, I want to repair my relationship with my family. I screwed it up, so I need to fix it."

"Great attitude. Be sure to talk with a counselor about what you've been through. Don't try to handle it all by yourself."

"Thanks, Liz. I guess I've learned that I can't do everything alone."

The third girl said she didn't recognize these two men, but she knew who her abductor was: a low life who lived in the small town of Hamlet, Indiana, where he worked at a golf course, cutting grass. She had been training as a bartender at the golf course, and because she was not a local, and living alone, this guy had taken her down to the same church in Little Spring. Liz explained this to the Indiana Trooper who came to take her home, and he said they'd have the man in custody for the young lady to identify. The Trooper said he would then accompany her home to Wanatah, where the girl's mother lived. All four girls had identified the minister, Albert Willis, Greg, and the two Donaldsons the evening before. These three women were willing to file charges against all four of them for wrongful imprisonment, and intent to employ them in illegal commercial sex acts.

The fourth girl, Leslie, came into the building with the older Kentucky Trooper described by Tillison. He had his hand on Leslie's shoulder and he led her to Liz, saying "You'll be okay now sweetheart. This lady will take good care of you."

The girl leaned her forehead against the Trooper's

shoulder and said, "Thank you for being so nice to me."

"No problem," he said. "I enjoyed our talk."

Liz smiled at the Trooper and mouthed, "Thank you." She knew that a vulnerable young person's interactions with an authority figure can be tense, even under good conditions. This officer had done a great job in settling Leslie's fears during their drive to Louisville.

Liz gave Leslie a warm hug and said, "I'm sorry I didn't offer last night, but you could have called my room to talk. I understand your sister is missing? We'll find her, and also arrest the guy who abducted you. I understand you're afraid it may be the same guy who's involved with your sister's disappearance?"

"Yes. My brother said he saw her with the guy that drove me over to Little Spring. I'm sure he took her, but I don't think he'd bring her over here knowing I was here. I heard him talking to a guy on the phone, during the drive down here, about a place in Huntington, but it was full. That's why he took me to Little Spring."

"Huntington, in West Virginia? We've worked with them before. But first, let's get this transporter into custody, so you can get over there to identify him. Once he knows he's facing trafficking charges, I'm sure he'll give us the location where he took your sister. Before we get you on the road, we'd like you to identify the people from Little Spring and the Donaldsons. Should we then call your brother, back in Independence? I'm sure he's worried about both of you."

"Thank you, Officer Trent. All of you have been so kind. I'm sorry for running this morning."

"It's Liz, by the way. But hey, we all understand. With what you've been through, and then finding out your sister is missing, I'm sure it feels like the world has crumbled around you. But now you're safe, and we will find your sister. And of course, that jerk back in Independence will be put away for a long time. I'll also have the State Trooper Detail over in your home county keep in touch with you and offer any help that they can."

"Thank you so much, for everything," Leslie said.

Liz personally saw to it that each of the girls got into the cars designated to take them home. She gave each of them a long hug and whispered something privately to each one. Tears were shed by all. Ashley, Adam, Curt and Steve watched her, and they all teared up, even Curt.

When the four girls had departed, Liz turned to Ashley. "This is why I seldom wear makeup or mascara. I seem to shed a lot of tears in this job and tears don't do well with mascara and makeup."

"Liz, I cannot believe you. You're not only good at police work, but I think you must be the most understanding, compassionate cop in the world. Sorry, that cop word came out again. How do you do it?" Ashley said.

"Well, I must admit, it gets tougher every time. I

don't think I can keep this up forever. It tears at your heart each time you see these girls in trouble, and it takes me longer each time to recover. It's a mixture of happiness to have found these four women, but I know that none of them will ever return to normal if they even had a normal life before. And by the way, after your help, you are now officially accepted as a police officer, so it's okay!

"This last girl was being raised by a brother, with no parents. That's the exact type of person these traffickers look for. No parents to raise the alarm. Then we have the girl working and living alone, away from home, with just a mother in her life. I've checked, and the mother never reported her as missing. The same goes for the two girls from Hammond because their families probably wouldn't realize they were missing until they didn't return home at the end of the school year. And both of them were taking summer classes. College kids don't call home like they used to. They text their parents, but the parents ignore texts, so the kids stop communicating. I know, because that was me, back in college.

"So, you see that trafficking isn't just a problem with the poor. It is a problem with all economic sectors, because even rich kids run away from home, and get picked up on the streets. It exists in the black and Hispanic communities, as well as white. The six people involved here, including you, Ashley, were from totally different economic and social backgrounds."

Adam said, "After this, I'm going to be much more

vigilant, looking for suspicious signs of girls who may be in trouble."

"Good," said Liz. "But don't forget young boys. Although not as prevalent, about 5%, one of every twenty young people abducted for sex, is a boy. Homeless boys on the street are very vulnerable. They have troubles at home and run away. But when they're cold or hungry, the sex-traffickers sweet-talk them into coming home with them. With a supply of drugs, like roofies, they lose any ideas of leaving."

"And moving forward, what will you need from us?" Curt asked.

"Well obviously, Ashley and Adam will be very involved in the depositions and the eventual trial. I don't think Henry and Larry will try to fight the charges, and it will be up to the judge whether or not Henry's cooperation will do him much good. I'm sure the minister thinks he can fight the charges, but he's not currently aware that Adam was posing as Larry, or that I am a police officer. He may now be aware of the Larry situation, but guys at that level always think they can fight the charges. I just wonder how many others at that church may have been involved.

"And as soon as you get back to Hammond, be sure to contact the East Chicago Police, and stay in touch with Indiana's investigator, Norman Jenkins. Those two girls who set up Julie will be charged in Indiana."

"What will happen to Leslie?" Ashley asked. "I'm very worried about her."

"There's only so much we can do," replied Liz. "Our

people will offer to find her counseling, but she is over eighteen, so we can only offer. I just hope we find her sister quickly."

"I think we need to get back to Hammond yet today, so we'd better get started," said Curt. "I cannot thank you enough, Liz. You made this terrible situation turn out acceptable. I'd love to say great, or happy, but that can't ever be the case in these situations, can it?"

"No, you're right. Just keeping everyone alive and with the least amount of trauma, is about the best we can ask for."

Ashley gave Liz a very long, sincere hug, and Adam did the same. Liz looked over at Curt and Steve and said, "No, you guys aren't getting away without a hug. Come on!"

Curt noticed that this time, Steve didn't blush. He seemed to enjoy hugging Liz.

Chapter 11

LIZ - LONG, SCARY ROAD TRIP

With Ashley and the others gone, I find myself in that position I've come to hate. Alone with my thoughts, my fears, and my lack of emotional support. I'm supposed to be this tough, indestructible person, but I also need and want so much to share my feelings with someone. Which is hard to do because I normally end up working these trafficking cases alone. I have back-up once I make a call for the bust, but I'm pretty much out there on the edge, face to face with either the transporters, the stable managers, or the pimps. I'm only twenty-seven, but I must admit, this work is wearing me thin, and I feel my emotional life getting more strained, the longer I work in this career. I haven't had a serious relationship in over two years, because I won't date other cops, and "normal" guys tend to drop me pretty fast after they find out what I do for a living. They probably think I'm way too experienced than they want to deal with. It's probably closer to the opposite because I'm so picky about the men I date.

I love my work for the results because I like to see the bad guys get what's coming to them. Most judges are tough on this crime because it involves a lot of under-aged kids, mostly girls. The judges usually have teenage grandchildren, and they can picture them being seduced over the internet or snatched off the streets. Traffickers don't care if their targets are rich or poor, black or white, as long as they look good. The business is run by creeps, and they recruit real scum to do the snatching for them.

What makes it hard to shut them down, however, are the other guys at the top. They're smart enough to keep changing their operations. What eventually tripped up that minister in Little Spring is that he let Henry and Larry make three abductions from the same college, using the same female accomplices, and the same apartment. Repetitive actions eventually raise suspicions, and luckily for the good guys, they bumped into Ashley and Adam Walters. Ashley in particular was a Police Investigator's dream, but Adam came in a close second! It's typical, and very understandable, for a victim in these crimes to just want to disappear. Just like Leslie tried to disappear. In Leslie's case, she was over eighteen, so we had no control over her and certainly couldn't force her to file charges.

Although, I am glad she did file charges against her abductor, even if it was because he had also abducted her fifteen-year-old sister. The local State Police Detachment, working out of the Ashland Post, had been investigating the trafficking around the Cincinnati, Ohio and Huntington/Charleston, West Virginia area, and they contacted Leslie to try finding her sister. Leslie happened to mention my name, and my boss received a call from the Sex Crimes Division Chief in Ashland, asking if they could 'borrow' me for help in this case.

The slimy creep who abducted Leslie, and now, her sister, wasn't admitting anything. Local Kentucky and West Virginia Police had suspicions about where girls were being delivered in the Huntington area, but they needed more than a suspicion to make a raid. They heard that I had a history of posing as a victim and asked if I'd be willing to help in their investigation.

I felt like I needed a rest after the stress of the situation with Ashley, but I had promised Leslie that 'we' would help her. 'We' was intended to mean the State Police, but it came out of my mouth, and now I feel a responsibility to help Leslie find her sister.

My boss asked if I was willing to assist, and I agreed. I drove to Ashland Kentucky to meet with the local Kentucky investigators and the West Virginia State Police. Without an escapee from a stable, called a runaway by their captors, the police could not obtain a warrant to make a raid. It's not illegal to dance at a Gentleman's Club, nor is it for the girls to perform lap dances. Although everyone assumes the club managers are pimping out the girls for additional sex acts, they claim that it is the girls who try to make extra money, and the pimps claim they were not aware.

Although it could be dangerous, the combined Kentucky/West Virginia task force was requesting that I act as a victim, allowing myself to be abducted and delivered to what they termed, a receiving station. That would be similar to the church we had raided in Little Spring. The West Virginia State Police said they had 'recruited' the services of a transporter from the Cincinnati area. It was another plea-bargain deal, so his charges would be less, or his sentence shortened. I hated these guys, but it was one of the only ways to get inside. This guy said he knew the operators in the Huntington operation, and he could tell them he had a girl to deliver. That girl was going to be ME!

I got my bag of smelly clothes out of my car, which not only had week-old sweat but now the urine smell from the recent operation with Ashley. I normally wash out the urine, but I hadn't had time to do that. I was introduced to the transporter, who turned out to be about 55 years old, with a sizeable beer gut, named Oscar. I was used to the 25-30-year-old guys, so this seemed unusual. He was instructed to drop me off and I was to witness the payment. As usual, I was then going to press my transmitter in my shoe, and the raid would occur.

This stable was located in the hills above Huntington. We drove up the winding road past the

Huntington airport. This drop-off was supposed to be at an old farmhouse. Oscar was talking constantly and changing subjects every 30-seconds. It appeared that he was more nervous than I was. Finally, he pulled into a long driveway that led to a dilapidated house, which looked like it hadn't been painted since the Civil War. I did my urinating trick after Oscar pulled me out of the back seat. Can't pee in his car if he's cooperating with the authorities.

Oscar led me up the steps, which I was afraid might cave in under Oscar's weight. He had to be well over 300-pounds. At the top of the stairs, Oscar knocked, and a woman, probably forty-five years old, dressed in shorts and a very revealing top, with no bra, answered the door.

Oscar said, "I brought that delivery from Cincy," Oscar told her. "This cutie should be worth more than the $3500, right?"

"Too late to bargain now," the woman said. Suddenly, I felt a sharp pain in my right buttock. I quickly began to blackout. Whatever it was, this stuff was working fast.

I woke up in a dark room with no lights and only a bit of moonlight coming through the window. I looked for my shoes, so I could push the transmitter but realized that I was naked. I had been stripped of my clothing, including my shoes. I tried to stand up, but whatever that woman had drugged me with, was still in my system. So, I crawled around the room looking for my clothes, particularly my shoes, but they were all gone. I found the door, it was locked. I had to use a toilet, really bad, and there wasn't one in the room, so I first whimpered, "Toilet, please," because all I could manage was a whimper. I heard nothing in return, so I kept saying, "Toilet, toilet..." until I finally heard footsteps.

"I'll let you use the toilet if you promise to be a good girl," the woman's voice said. It sounded like the woman who had talked to Oscar.

"I can't stand up. I'm too dizzy," I told her.

"Well good, so I guess you won't give me any trouble then." I heard her unlock the door.

"Where are my clothes?" I asked her. "I don't like being naked."

"I burned those nasty things. They smelled terrible like you pissed in them too. Didn't that guy let you out to pee?"

"No, he didn't," I told her. Can you give me some clothes?"

"If you promise to be nice, I'll let you shower first. Don't want you smelling up my car during the drive. Had to put you in the trunk to get you here. Didn't want you in my car, smelling like that. How old are you, sweetheart?"

"Seventeen," I lied. At least that's what my co-workers said I looked like.

"That's a perfect age. Wait 'til they see what I found for them."

"Why am I here?" I asked.

"No questions for now, sweetheart. You'll find out later."

She let me in the bathroom where I used the toilet and took a long shower. I started to feel better after the shower, so I just sat in the old tub with the shower running. I was also afraid to stand up, but by the time I got out of the shower and was dressed, my dizziness started to disappear and my thoughts a little clearer.

The woman hadn't mentioned my transmitter, so it had probably been burned with my shoes. Therefore, she couldn't suspect that I was with the police, but I wasn't sure. I was still getting dressed when the woman came into the bathroom with a syringe in her hand.

"No more drugs, please," I said pleading with her. "It made me so dizzy."

"Yes, that last dose was too much. You're just a little slip of a thing. This is only a half-dose, just to be sure you stay a nice girl." With that, she jabbed me in my same buttock. This time, I felt my senses deadening, but I was still able to hear, and I could walk, but felt very shaky.

"Let's go, sweetheart," she said. "Times a-wastin' and people to see." It was bothering me that she kept calling me sweetheart when I knew what she had planned for me.

"I'm hungry," I told her. "Can I have something to eat?"

"If you be a nice girl, I might get you a hamburger later. For now, we gotta' get on the road."

She led me outside and I could see that this was not the farm where Oscar had dropped me off. I didn't know if Oscar knew what was happening, but he had to have seen this woman pop the syringe into my butt. He obviously got paid and just left me there. He knew about the transmitter, but it seems like he didn't tell the woman. If she knew I was a cop, I might be on my way to being dumped in the Ohio River. But from the look of things, it seemed Oscar had just bailed out with his money. All I could do now was hope the West Virginia Troopers had seen this woman load me in her trunk and move me.

This organization sure seemed to be smarter than the ones back in Little Spring. The drop-off location was just that. I saw nobody there other than this woman. Of course, I wasn't conscious for long. And the place where I woke up also seemed deserted, so the managers kept themselves out of the abduction and delivery parts of the operation. Now I had to figure out where I was headed and try to slow her down.

The woman put me into the back seat. She had one handcuff coming out of the middle of the seat, where the seat belt buckle should have been, and locked my left wrist into the cuff and closed the door.

"I think I'm going to be sick," I told her, as she got into the driver's seat.

"Must still have given you too much. I'll lighten the

dose again next time," she said. "Here, take this, and don't barf in my car." She threw me a plastic bag.

I didn't need to vomit, but I did a good job of letting her know I was serious, and I was able to get a little bile to come up. "I need some food, or I'll get sick again," I told her.

"You won't starve, and like I told you, I'll get you a hamburger if you're a good girl. Now just sit quiet. Maybe you'll go to sleep."

As we started driving, I could tell we were no longer up past the Huntington airport where Oscar had taken me. I saw her cross a bridge over the Ohio River, and I saw the 'Welcome to Ohio' sign. I then started to realize I was in big trouble, and no wonder the Kentucky and West Virginia Task Force wasn't finding any of these girls. This drop-off had nothing to do with a local sex ring, and I had no idea where I was headed.

She was taking Interstate Highways, but when I saw signs for Columbus, Ohio, she exited and stopped to gas up her car. It was on a side street, at an old service station. While the gas was pumping, she reached across from the left rear door and stuck another syringe in my butt. At least, this one was on my left side. "Just a light dose this time," she said, "do you have to pee? If you promise to be nice, I'll take you into the restroom. Then we'll go to that drive-thru across the street, and I'll get you a hamburger."

This could have been my chance to escape, but whatever drug she was using had me in such a state that I doubted I could walk straight, no less run. She pulled into a parking spot around the side of the station. There was only a men's room out there, and I supposed the women's restroom was inside. She went in with me, and she used the toilet first. Then she had to sit me down on the seat because I was wobbling so much. On the way out, a man was waiting to go inside.

The woman told him, "She's a bit drunk. I didn't want her to barf inside the station."

I wanted to say something, but the drug was doing its business, and I couldn't even speak. She put me back into the car and reattached my handcuff. Then she drove across the street. I heard her order a bunch of food, and after we pulled away from the window, she threw a bag into the back seat. I tried to grab it, but it fell on the floor. I tried to reach for it, and I passed out again.

When I awoke this time, I saw we were on Highway-23, and I saw a sign saying, 'Findlay 23-miles.' I thought, 'Holy Crap, she's headed to Toledo.'

I was able to reach the bag on the floor and found one plain hamburger inside. As I was eating it, I asked her for something to drink. She handed me a paper cup, which was now nearly empty and already warm. I must have been asleep for a long time. "Not giving you much to drink. We have a long way to go. Only one more potty stop along the way."

"Where are you taking me?" I asked.

"Enough questions, sweetheart."

The next thing I saw was a sign for Highway I-94, to Ann Arbor and Detroit. This was by no means a local operation, and I was very worried. I was sure the Troopers were doing a good job trying to locate me around West Virginia, maybe even in Ohio, but now we were in Michigan. I was supposed to be a well-trained sex-trafficking investigator, and here I was, drugged and helpless in the back of a car, heading to Michigan, or maybe beyond. I didn't think she dared take me to Canada, but right then, even that wouldn't surprise me.

After driving for quite some distance, the woman finally pulled into a roadside park, apparently to use the restroom. She opened the rear door, and again she was holding a syringe. I begged her not to give me more, but she just stuck me again. No wonder these girls who get abducted don't get away. I thought I could handle this, but now I was scared. She may be reducing the doses, but if she kept this up, I was sure it had to be messing me up.

There were a lot of truckers in this rest stop, and I was weaving around, unable to talk. When they stared at us, the woman just said, "Drunk little shit. I'm taking her home. My husband will teach her a lesson this time." Even if I wanted to object, I couldn't get the words out. This damn drug of hers was some-thing else.

Again, I passed out in the back of the car, and the next time I woke up, some guy was dragging me out of the car. "Sweet young thing you got this time. Where'd she come from?" he asked.

"The guy said he found her in Cincinnati. She

says she's seventeen. Probably not a virgin, but a real looker. You like?"

"Yes, I like it. Don't get many like this one. How much you have to pay?"

"Just the standard $3500. The guy wanted more, but I told him it was too late to negotiate."

"Good job, Darla. You know what you're doin'," he said.

"What do you plan on doing with her, Luke?"

"I think I'll save her for private parties. She'll bring more once the word gets around. I won't waste this talent at one of the clubs."

"Okay, you know what to do from here on. Pay me in the usual way. Can I stay in one of your rooms until morning? Then I'm headed home. I may have another one for you next week."

"Sounds good, Darla. Looks like you have her really drugged up though. You need to watch that stuff when they're skinny ones like this. You might be delivering a corpse if you're not careful."

"Yes, I had her down to nearly a quarter-dose for the pee-breaks, but she still passed out each time. I showered her off back home."

"You still live in that little burgh? Buffalo Hills?"

"Buffalo Creek. But sure. Nobody questions me bringing these drunk girls home with me. They all think I'm counseling them."

"I suppose. But I couldn't live in a small town like that."

"No stores or other such things to attract attention.

You've never had any trouble with the girls I bring you, so stop complaining. I'm keeping both of us safe. You can keep this cold Michigan weather, and all these hillbillies working at the car plants."

"Yup. And most of those hillbillies came from down your way. They keep my clubs profitable, and girls like this one keep the managers happy. She's going to be a money-maker."

"She sure doesn't look brain-dead like some of these girls. Wait until you see her after the drugs wear off. She has a twinkle in her eyes."

"Okay, Darla. Room #12 is open for you, and on the opposite end of the motel from the party girls. I know you don't like being disturbed by them. I'll keep this one in the room with me, in case she gets any bright ideas to run. When's the last time you stopped to let her pee?"

"Better do that before you cuff her to the bed. It's been a couple hours, down by Ann Arbor."

"Right. Then I can inspect the goods while she does her business."

"She does have a nice body for such a skinny one. You'll be impressed, Luke."

I was surprised that they had talked so freely in front of me. Then again, in their minds, I was just some random 17-year-old street kid. Now, I just hoped I could remember the details of their conversation when the effects of the drug wore off. I sure was looking forward to having the West Virginia Troopers pay a visit to Miss Darla.

Chapter 12

BRAINWASHING

Luke led me into the office of what appeared to be a small, 1960's style motel. I was still wobbly from all the drugging by Darla, but my mind was starting to work better again. I saw Darla head down to the end of the string of rooms. I only saw three pick-ups parked in front of the rooms. Luke led me to a room behind the office, where I saw another woman, maybe thirty-five. She had bleached blond hair and heavy makeup. "So, Darla brought another one. This one looks a lot better than that last wench she brought. What are you going to do with this one, and don't tell me you're keeping her for yourself?" I noticed this woman wasn't just joking. It sounded like Luke had been fooling around with some of his others.

"No, I don't like using the talent. Then they don't like the customers as much, and the customers get mad."

"Don't give yourself so much credit. You're not as great in the sack as you think you are."

"Look who's talking. I rescued you off the streets and kept you for myself. Now you're complaining? I could start selling your ass, sweet cheeks!"

I was liking the sounds of this. Luke and his woman, I sure wouldn't say his girlfriend, are not getting along. If I can just find a way to use this, somehow.

"Darla said she hasn't peed since she crossed the state line, down near Ann Arbor. She suggested that I let her pee before we put her to bed," Luke explained.

"And I know your routine. You're going to watch her drop her drawers, just for business reasons, right? You need to inspect the merchandise."

"You can come and watch me if you want."

"No, and spoil your fun? Just don't screw her, or I'm leaving this time."

Luke led me into the toilet, and as much as I hated it, I did sit down. I needed to go sooner or later and doing it in bed was probably not smart. "Pull the shirt up, so I can see what you got," Luke said. Again, I figured I'd better comply. Luke took my breasts in his hands but was surprisingly gentle, "Not bad for seventeen. Are you a virgin?"

I shook my head. "Where am I? When can I go home?"

"This is home now, baby. I'll treat you just fine. I know that Darla was kinda mean, but I'll take good care of you. I'm a nice guy and I'm not mean."

"No more drugs, please. They make me sick."

"If you promise to stay with me, and won't run away, I promise no more drugs. We'll have a lot of fun, throw parties with my friends, and you'll be better here than you were before. Cincinnati, right?

"Yah, Cincy."

"Is your family there in Cincy?"

"No. Mom died. I never saw my father. I've been on the streets for six months since Mom is gone."

"See? You weren't happy before, and the guys on the streets probably treated you bad. I'm going to be nice to you. All the food and booze you want, party with my friends, and everyone will be happy. Sound good?"

"I guess," I said. Here I've wondered just how these operators kept their girls from running. I thought it was all drugs and threats, but Luke was showing me how it happens. He was planning to keep me happy, at least his version of happy. If I had been abused at home, or out on the streets, I would think this was a fantastic outcome. Trafficking and sex slavery weren't involved. He was being nice, and all I needed to do was keep his friends happy. Experiencing this tactic firsthand was enlightening, but this wasn't my idea of being happy. Now I just had to find a way to escape.

As soon as Luke brought me out of the bathroom, the blond started in on him again. "So, did you like what you saw? Nice tits? Did you squeeze 'em real nice? Good round ass? Did you even check out the equipment?"

"Damn it, Shauna, don't upset her. She's a nice girl and she's had a tough life. We're going to treat her right, so knock off the tough talk. You'll upset her. I told her she'd be happy here with us."

Shauna stomped off into the next room, and I assumed she was very upset. Luke gave me a couple bottles of water and said we'd have a nice breakfast the next morning. He said if I ate now, the drugs might make me sick.

I said, "No more shots, please."

"No," he said. "But I need to cuff you to the bed or Shauna will get mad. You can see that Shauna doesn't like me much anymore. Maybe you and I can be a couple. How would you like that?"

"Maybe," I mumbled.

"Okay, baby. Think about that. Sleep well, and I'll see you in the morning."

Then Luke cuffed one of my wrists to the bed, actually kissed me on the forehead, turned off the lights, and went into the next room. Even I was confused, so I could just imagine how a real runaway would feel at this point. I wasn't sure if Luke and Shauna were fighting or if it was all an act to make me think he was going to be my protector. I had slept a lot in the car, due to the drugs, so I couldn't fall asleep. About forty-five minutes later, after just hearing whispering from the next room, I then heard my answer. Luke and Shauna were making mad, passionate love, and it wasn't like two people who had been fighting just an hour before. It had all been an act for my benefit. Very smart!The next morning, Luke came out of his room, uncuffed me, and let me go to the toilet by myself. When I came out of the bathroom, he was waiting for me. "I kicked Shauna out last night. How would you like to stay here with me? Here, sit down. I hope you like bacon. How do you like your eggs? Scrambled okay, or I can fry some for you?"

"I guess so. Scrambled is fine."

"Now, you don't have to sleep with me. I'm just trying to be nice to you. Get used to the place. Just relax, watch TV, catch up on your sleep. I'll have one of my friends pick up some new clothes for you. Maybe some makeup. But you're pretty, so you probably don't need makeup. And by the way, do you like steak, chicken, pasta? I'll get us some good stuff to eat."

He was laying it on thick. Luke was a nice-looking guy. I was thinking maybe late thirties. If it wasn't for his choice of trade, I might have even been attracted to him. He was short, maybe five-nine, looked like he worked out occasionally, and had well-groomed hair, which seemed to be unusual in this business. He even had a pleasant smile, which he was continually using on me.

I assumed that Shauna had gone out a back door before Luke came in to continue his propaganda. I could just see how Luke was able to manipulate young girls into trusting him. What worried me was how Luke was going to introduce the sexual favors. It didn't sound like he expected me to satisfy him, but sooner than later, he was going to expect some return on his investment. Then, what was I going to do?

The nice treatment went on for two days. Luke kept the doors locked, and I saw the locks needed a key from both sides. He occasionally went out to the office, and I'd hear him talking. Sometimes it seemed like actual travelers, but this wasn't that great of a motel. I could overhear some loud conversations, and Luke would say, "She's waiting for you in number-three. Did you want a few hours or all night like last time?" Occasionally the customer had not pre-arranged his visit and Luke would say, "What are you looking for tonight? You name it and I've probably got it." One time I heard the customer ask if there were any boys available, and Luke said, "Not tonight, but give me some notice before your next trip and I'll be sure to have a nice young one for you." This guy was a real operator, and much more professional than most I'd encountered.

Chapter 13

THE REAL STORY

On my third day with Luke and Shauna, Luke made me breakfast. He was being so sweet, that I had a feeling the time had come. "You know, baby. You've never told me your name, and I don't blame you. I know you want to leave all those bad times behind you. Why don't we just pick a name that you like? Any ideas? Your choice, but I kinda like Sasha. It sounds like Russian. Would you like me to call you that?"

"I like Sasha," I said. Knowing full well that he had some guy wanting a Russian girl, so it was going to be Sasha.

"Tonight, for dinner, I have a friend stopping by. I bought some nice steaks, and I had someone buy a nice set of new clothes for you. We can have a fancy dinner and some drinks with my friend. You don't talk much, but my friend won't mind. Just be friendly to him, okay?"

I nodded.

"If you don't talk a lot, he won't realize that you don't have much of a Russian accent," Luke said with a small hint of laughter in his voice."

"Okay," I said. Now I was worried. The time had come, and being nice over dinner wasn't going to be the end of this evening. Just what the hell was I going to do?

The customer showed up around six. I guess I was expecting some rough-looking dude, with his hands all over me. Instead, the guy looked more scared than I was, and if anything, he was being polite, as if he was on a real date. I suspected that Luke wasn't going to let me be entirely myself, even if he had done his best to seduce me with kindness. Luke asked the man what he was drinking, and the guy requested a brandy, neat. Luke asked me, "And Sasha, what about you?" I answered, "The same. I like brandy." In my peripheral vision, I noticed that Luke dropped something, probably a date-rape drug into one glass, and he gave that glass to me. When Luke went to get the steaks and bring them to the table, I distracted the customer and switched glasses.

While eating, the customer started looking drowsy, which I knew was the effect of the drug. I tried to mimic his actions, so Luke would assume I was drugged, and the customer was just getting drunk from the brandy. The customer said, "So, Sasha, I hear you are new to this country. You came from Russia?"

I saw Luke look at me and smile, nodding his head. I said, "Yes. Very new."

The man went on, "Can we go somewhere to talk? I'd like to know more about you."

Luke spoke up, "Why there's an empty room down in number-five. Sasha would love to talk with you. Be nice to her, Dave. She's just a young immigrant girl, you understand."

"I'm a real gentleman, I'll have you know. Shall we go, Sasha?"

Luke whispered in my ear, "Be nice to Dave. He's a good friend, and he looks a little drunk."

I stumbled towards the door, with Dave on my arm. At this point, I wasn't sure if he was leading me, or if I was holding him up. Dave already had the key to number five in his pocket, so it was obvious that he knew what was supposed to happen. As soon as the door closed, I was pretty sober, having spilled most of my three brandies. Poor Dave, with five brandies and my drugged glass as well, was dropping fast.

"I said, "Dave, can you drive me to another place? I need to leave."

"I'd love to go with you, Sasha, but I don't have a car. I came in a taxi. Where do you want to go? I can have Luke call us a taxi."

"That's okay, Dave. You're a nice guy, but you shouldn't be going to places like this. Why don't you lay down on the bed? I have something I want to show you."

"Should I take my clothes off first?"

"No, for this show, it won't matter."

Dave laid down and was nearly passed out. No wonder date rape victims sometimes never remember what happened to them. I tore the pillowcases into strips and tied Dave's arms and legs to the bedposts. As a nice touch, I kissed Dave on the forehead, leaving a nice lipstick mark.

I was sure that Luke had cameras in the parking lot, he'd be stupid not to, so the very small, sliding window in the bathroom was my only escape. I wasn't sure that even I could fit through that small half of the window if I just slid it open, and I was afraid that breaking the glass would alert Luke to my escape. So I got one of the bath towels to protect my hands and I pulled the window, trying to force it out of its frame. It took several tries, I didn't have a lot of weight behind my efforts, but the window finally gave in, and I was able to pull it out of the wall. When the glass broke on the bathroom floor, I heard Dave say, "Are you okay, Sasha? Come back to bed and show me what you have planned." I nearly laughed but got right back to business. I knew I had to get out of there, and quickly.

Standing on the toilet seat, I jumped up to that small window opening repeatedly before getting a grasp. I was able to grab the sides of the window and pull myself through. I took a good tumble onto the gravel below. I scraped my knees and elbows, but I was out. I ripped the nice dress Luke had bought, and if I had been any larger, I'd never have gotten through. I wouldn't even have the dress to remember my time with Luke, I thought. I didn't want to lose my sense of humor at a time like this.

The back of the motel was on a long, dark, dirty alley. I got to the first lighted street and saw a service station about two blocks away. I walked there and asked the attendant if he had a phone.

"Not for personal use," he said.

I thought of having him call "911" but I needed to get the goods on Luke's operation first. A local police raid would end up with nothing.

"Where am I, anyway?" I asked the attendant.

"This is a Speedway station. What do you think?" he said, somewhat irritated.

"No, I mean what city am I in?"

"You don't even know what city you're in? Are you on drugs or something?"

Finally, I figured some honesty would help, so I told him, "I was kidnapped and drugged down in West Virginia. I just escaped, and I need to get help. Can I please use your phone?"

"Maybe I should call '911' then," he said.

"Please don't. I know I don't look like it but I'm a Kentucky State Police officer, and I was tracking some sex traffickers. I got in the way, and they drugged me and brought me here. And just where is here?"

"You're in Flint, Michigan. That story is just too crazy not to be true. I can let you make a call if you tell me where to call."

"We can't call the police yet. I need to get help

first. Could you find a phone number for Curt Steiner in Cadillac?"

"Cadillac's a couple hours away. Shouldn't I call the police?"

"I'll tell you the whole story, but first, can you see if you can find that number? Thank you."

Chapter 14

BACK TO SAFETY

Lois Steiner was laughing hysterically. It left me stumped for a moment. The station attendant had managed to call Directory Assistance on his cell phone, and they gave him Curt Steiner's number. I was surprised to hear a woman answer, so I asked her if she was Mrs. Steiner. Then I explained to her that although she didn't know me, she may have heard my name.

"I'm Officer Elizabeth Trent, Kentucky State Police."

That's when she burst out laughing.

"So, you do exist?" she finally said, when she was calmer.

"I do exist, Mrs. Steiner, but this is not a social call. I'm in Flint, Michigan, and I'm in big trouble. Can I bother your husband to get some help?"

"Well, I have Curt's phone because he happens to be in the hospital. Nothing serious, just minor surgery.

But he wanted his phone answered while he was out of commission, so that's why I answered. However, I understand that you had a date with my son, Steve, and he's in the next room, playing cards with the kids before bed. Let me get Steve."

"I hope Curt and Steve told you, it wasn't a real date."

"I trust both of them, and after I realized it wasn't some practical joke, they explained it quite well. You're off the hook, at least until I meet you."

I was about to say thank you, but Steve came on the line, "Liz? This is you? What's up? Mom said something about trouble."

"Steve, I'm in Flint, Michigan. This time, I was kidnapped. Long story for later. I've escaped, but I need to contact my superiors and plan what to do. I can't do all of that from this kind man's phone, and I'm stuck here with no car, no phone, and no ID. I understand that you're two hours away, but I need to get away from here quickly. My captors are not far away, and pretty soon, they'll know I escaped."

"Let me talk to the attendant, Liz."

Steve talked to the attendant, and then came back on the phone. "I'm leaving now and heading for Bay City. I'm ordering an Uber to take you there. You'll be going to see a lady named Annette. She is the partner of one of our tug captains. I'll meet you there, and I'll let Annette know what's happening."

"I'll pay for all of this, Steve. Thank you. For the first time in my career, I was scared."

"Hey, I'm just paying you back for helping us. I'll see you at Annette's place in a couple hours."

I was about to hang up with Steve when the Uber pulled up. I thanked the attendant for trusting and helping me. I promised to come back and take him to lunch after all things got sorted out. Then I asked him if he could keep this whole incident quiet until he saw it in the news. He said, "If you promise to tell me everything over lunch."

The Uber driver seemed to be happy with this ride, which he said was going to be about 50 miles.

"Your boyfriend also gave me a nice tip. Be sure to thank him," he said, smiling at me through the rear-view mirror. I smiled back.

"Did he say he was my boyfriend?"

"Not really. I just assumed so, because he said you were valuable cargo."

"And he said that?"

"Not lying, young lady. I could tell that he likes you."

I wasn't sure where this attraction between us was taking me. I seriously thought I'd probably never see him again. He was six years younger, that didn't bother me, but I could tell that his dad was concerned, and if I met his mother, she might tell Steve to stay away from me.

The ride went much faster than I expected. When we arrived, the driver said he'd wait out front until I signaled him to leave, which was better than Uber drivers in Louisville. I went to the door of a nice two-story townhome, rang the bell, and was greeted by a beautiful smiling lady.

"I'm Annette Sullivan," she said, introducing herself. I waved to the Uber driver and went in.

"So, you are the famous Liz I've been hearing about! I can't believe you're here. I understand that you'll need to make a few critical phone calls, so we can talk later."

"You're sure you don't mind?"

"Absolutely. And if you want some privacy, I can close the door to my office."

"I don't mind if you hear, but we need to keep this quiet until it breaks on the news. You'll understand once you hear the conversations."

"Then I'd better tell you, I'm a columnist for the local paper. But I do know how to keep my mouth shut."

"Having you hear all of this may be a good thing. Does your paper cover Flint?"

"We cover most of Central Michigan, and we have sharing agreements well beyond Michigan."

"Wonderful. Then maybe take notes, and after the fireworks, we can collaborate on that column you will want to write."

Annette grabbed a pen and pad from her desk and sat on the love seat in her office while I sat behind her desk.

My first phone call was to my boss at home in Louisville. I even thought I heard him getting emotional, which the man just never did. He thought that

I had been killed. He gave me the home number of the head of the Joint Kentucky/West Virginia Task Force that I had been helping. But I reminded my boss that it was close to midnight, and he said, "Trust me, Liz. He hasn't been sleeping much since you disappeared. He will love hearing from you."

"Hey boss, please let Tillison and the FBI guys know that I'm okay. And by the way, I'll need some time off after this one."

"Does Paid Medical Leave sound okay?" he said.

"Yes."

Next, I called the captain at home in Ashland, Kentucky. I could tell by his quick answer that he had not been sleeping. "Captain Kelly, this is Liz. I'm okay." The man screamed, telling his wife that I was on the phone.

"I've been so worried, Liz. When the transmitter wasn't activated, we waited another hour and then sent a plainclothes guy to that house. Nobody was there. We found Oscar in a bar in Huntington. He said he didn't know what to do when that woman slammed that syringe into your leg, so he took her money and skedaddled."

"It was a scary, few days, Chief. But I have some real stories to tell. I'll write down the names, where that woman lives, and everything about the place I was held. I was inside a real brothel in Flint, Michigan."

"Oh, God. You didn't have to...?"

"Came close, Chief. But my experience paid off. I'm now with friends in Bay City, Michigan. Call me at this number when you get to the office in the morning, so we can decide how to move forward. By now, I assume my captors know I've escaped. I didn't want to involve the local police, so you'll need to contact someone in Michigan and the local FBI office. I can work with them to make the bust on the Flint operation. He's a smooth operator, I'll tell you. I always wondered how these girls get duped into cooperating, but I saw it first-hand. He became my friend, and he just asked me to keep his friends happy. I can see how it works."

"I'm just so happy that you're safe, Liz. I was thinking the worst and beating myself up for putting you in that position."

"Well, Chief, I'll be sending you some unusual expenses for telephone calls, Uber rides, and a lunch for a gas station attendant. Just don't object, okay?"

"Not a problem, Officer Trent. Just submit them."

"Talk to you in the morning, Chief."

I hung up the phone and finally let it all hit me. That's when I felt the tears. Annette saw the tears and came over to sit by me. Then she pulled me close, put her arms around me, and allowed me to sob into her chest. I had come close to having a first-hand experience of what these girls go through, and it shook me up. It's hard to deal with these emotions alone. Nobody to go to as a normal, scared woman. I'm supposed to be the tough State Trooper, so I never have a chance to dump my emotions on anyone. I was glad to finally have a shoulder to cry on, away from judging eyes.

Chapter 15

STEVE AND LIZ

Annette sat next to Liz with her mouth open. "I know that all had to be true. It sounds like a movie script. Just amazing, and you are lucky to be alive."

"I figured I'd be okay, as long as they didn't find out I was a cop. I was afraid the delivery guy in West Virginia, Oscar might spill the beans, and then the lady who transported me didn't find my transmitter, which was lucky. What worried me most was the drugs she kept injecting. I don't know how long I was out from that first one, but she threw me into the trunk of her car and drove me to another house, and I woke up after dark. I think she was scared she'd killed me, so she reduced the dose by half, and then half again."

"And then the place in Flint," Annette said. "I guess we all know there are brothels in most cities, but I guess we all assume they only use willing prostitutes. I've heard about human trafficking, because of my job, but I thought those places only existed in Detroit or Chicago, not right here."

Just then, Annette's doorbell rang. "I'll bet that's Steve. You should have heard him on the phone when he told me you were coming. That young man is smitten with you, Liz."

"We're just friends."

Annette smirked at that. Then she walked off to answer the door.

"Is she here? Tell me she's okay," were Steve's first words.

Liz came around the corner into the hall and said, "I thought you knew that I could take care of myself."

"Well, a couple hours ago, you didn't sound that way on the phone" Steve gave Liz a very lingering, tight hug.

"You probably heard me at one of the lowest points in my career. I was worried that if the guy broke loose, the pimp was going to walk into that gas station with another syringe of that stuff. Maybe you did hear a little fear in my voice about then."

"So, what's the plan? I'm at your disposal. My dad cleared my schedule to help you. My mom called the hospital to tell him you were in trouble, and he said you were my job until you told me to get lost. That's a quote, according to my mother."

"I'm sure I'll need to talk with the Ashland Kentucky Troopers in the morning. You remember Leslie, the girl from Independence? We were trying to find her sister, but this time I got nabbed. I'll tell you the details tomorrow because Annette has heard it all already. Then, we may be needed in Flint, when the FBI raids that place where I was being held. I don't think he'll suspect a raid, because I think I played my part well, and when he finds his client tied to the bed, he'll just assume I escaped and was running back to Cincinnati."

"Oh my God! All this happened since I saw you last? That is less than a week. How do you keep doing this and remain sane?" Steve asked.

"I have to admit, this one has made me think seriously about my career choice. I love the high I get when things go right, like right now. But there were times over the last several days when I knew the tension is not healthy. And then the drugs they gave me, I'm sure they've shortened my life a little."

"I have three kids who are going to wake me up in the morning, so I'm heading to bed," Annette said at that point. "There's white wine in the fridge, or iced tea if you prefer, in case you want to talk awhile. There's a guest room and a sofa. The options are yours."

"Annette, thank you so much for this," Liz said. "I bet you never thought you'd hear all of this tonight."

"As I said, Liz. I want an exclusive story out of this. I'm hoping we can heighten awareness of this trafficking, which exists right under our noses. I'll see you guys in the morning."

"And Annette, remember that Captain Kelly only has your phone number. He'll be calling early."

"The kids will be up at six-thirty, so not to worry."

"And my thanks too, Annette," said Steve.

"Hey, as Stormi always reminds me, we're part of

the Strauss/Steiner family. And family helps family, right?"

"But I'm not family," Liz said.

"You haven't heard what Ashley, Adam, this young man, and even Curt have said about you. I think you've been adopted into the family, without your knowledge."

Liz and Steve each had a glass of wine after Annette went off to bed. They talked some about her recent drama.

"I understand that I can get into Law School at the University of Michigan. I checked it out. What do you think?"

"Are you serious? What about your love of police work?"

"Well, I'd still be working against the same bad guys, but helping the police to convict them instead of catching them. My field experience will make me a great prosecutor."

"I think it will. Does our friendship have anything to do with this idea?" Steve asked.

"Only if you want to keep looking into the possibility."

"I do, I'm just worried that you might end up thinking I'm too young for you."

"Look at it in reverse, Steve. Do you think I'm too old for you? And if you think I have a lot of experience with men, you're wrong. So, I'm not saying we should make any commitments, and in case you think I'm leading up to a request for us to share a bed tonight, the answer is NO! But I want to learn more about you. How about you?"

"All I've thought about this week was you, Liz. Sure, I was first attracted to your looks, but then I saw your confidence and caring for the girls you rescued. This isn't just a job for you. I can see that you care about what happens afterward. That impressed me even more. So, yes. I would like to get to know you better.

"Okay then. That's settled. Once I clear up all the messes I've gotten myself into the last few days, I'm going to apply for Law School at the U of M. That gives us a year until you graduate, and then we'll see what happens. But for now, I'm sorry, but you get the sofa, and I get the guest room. I've had a bad day, and I need some sleep."

"Wait! Why the U of M?" Steve asked.

"I found out it's the only undergrad program for Naval Architecture, other than Webb, and I didn't think you were going to school in New York. Am I right?" Liz quipped.

"So, you're planning on stalking me in Ann Arbor?"

"Call it what you like. Good night, and thanks again for rescuing me."

Morning came way too early. Steve was wakened by three excited kids, wondering what he was doing in their house. They knew Steve from company gatherings but finding him asleep on their sofa was exciting.

Annette soon followed and apologized for the early wake-up call. She asked if he needed coffee and he gladly said, "Yes please!"

"Do we wake up Liz or let her sleep," Annette asked.

"I think she's going to have a busy day," Steve said. "Let's let her sleep as long as we can."

"Think again," Liz said from the top of the stairs. "I'm already showered and waiting for that phone call. I hope you don't mind that I made myself at home in your guest bath?"

"I'm happy you did," said Annette. "Did you find everything you needed?"

"I'm fine, but I'm going to need the guys in Kentucky to pay for some clothes. All of my ID and credit cards are in our Ashland office. That was supposed to be a one-day sting, ending in a raid. Didn't go as planned."

"I can pay for some clothes," Steve said.

"Not a chance, my friend. I can just see the look on your mother's face if she saw those charges. I can work it out with my recent boss, the guy in Ashland."

Annette's phone rang and she answered, "Yes Captain Kelly. She's right here." And she handed her phone to Liz.

Annette and Steve chatted while Liz discussed how things would happen. Liz provided the Buffalo Creek location and Darla's name, as well as the fact that she was believed to be counseling young girls and using that as the cover for her activities. Then they heard her ask about contacts she needed with the FBI in

Detroit. There were State Police Posts in both Flint and Bay City. Captain Kelly said he requested an initial meeting in Bay City, to avoid any possibility of alerting their trafficker that he could be in trouble. Then Liz reminded Captain Kelly that she had no money, no ID, and she needed clothes. Liz was surprised when Captain Kelly told her that her things were on the way. The Kentucky, Ohio, and Michigan State Police had all cooperated since he had received her call last night, and the last report was the final car was about an hour from Bay City. He just needed an address where to deliver her belongings.

"I assume my cell phone is included?" Liz asked.

"Included and fully charged," Kelly said.

"Then please have the Bay City State Police Post call me with meeting instructions. I don't want this joker in Flint to fly the coop. And finally, Captain Kelly, remember that the original plan behind this operation was to find Leslie's sister. I know the guy who snatched both of them was in Independence, and he said he delivered the sister to Huntington. I'm hoping we might find her in Flint, but all we know so far is that the guy from Independence delivered Leslie's sister to Huntington. We can hope she went to this same Darla woman, so lean on her heavy to find Leslie's sister. I promised her we'd find her sister."

"Yes, Liz. That is priority one, now that I know you are safe."

Annette's daughter came running into the kitchen, "Momma, there's a police car outside."

"I think he's here to see Liz. You can go to the door and let him in. Say hi, and welcome," Annette said. "The kids will remember today for a long time. Finding Steve on the sofa and an unexpected house guest, and now a policeman at our front door."

Annette's daughter guided the Trooper into the kitchen, carrying two large duffel bags. He said, "Special delivery for Officer Trent. I was told she looks like seventeen, so that must be you." And he then handed Liz her phone.

"Okay, who told you to use the 'seventeen' greeting?" Liz laughed.

"That message was transferred from car to car, Kentucky, to Ohio, to Michigan, and I'm the third car in Michigan. All done verbally, off the radio, to be sure nobody overheard if they listened in. Apparently, you have a big fan club, Officer Trent."

"No, they just know I'd be real upset if they screw up this investigation."

"I've also been told to escort you to the Bay City Post offices. Can I do that now?"

"Officer, I was just about to serve them breakfast. Can I offer you some coffee, while they sit down and eat?" Annette said.

"I'd love a cup of coffee. And can I presume that you are Annette Sullivan? I recognize your picture from your column in the paper. My wife will be jealous that I met you. We both love your columns."

"Guilty as charged. Though that is a sick attempt at humor," as Annette laughed.

After Liz and Steve gulped down the last of their coffee, Liz asked, "Would you mind if my friend, Steve Steiner, came along to this meeting? Steve was involved in the trafficking sting we made in suburban Louisville last week, so I'd like him to come along."

"He's certainly welcome to come to the Post. You can check with our captain about him being in the meeting. I'm back out on the road after I get you to the meeting."

"Okay, we'll follow you in Steve's truck, That's it, right in front of your squad."

"Sounds good," the Trooper said. "Great to meet you, Miss Sullivan."

"Same here, Officer."

Liz then turned to Annette to let her know they'd let her know what happens. "If we're headed straight to Flint, we'll come back this way. Steve doesn't know it yet, but I'm going to Cadillac with him, so I can meet his mother. About now, she's probably really wondering about me and my intentions." Both Annette and Steve gave Liz a surprised look after that statement.

"And please remember to keep all of this quiet until I tell you."

"No problem," Annette said.

Chapter 16

ANOTHER STING & BUST

Steve Steiner's name showed up on the reports that both the FBI and the Michigan State Police had received, relative to the sting and raid at the Gentlemen's Club the previous week in Kentucky. So, he was invited to sit in on the meeting at the Bay City Post. Liz received the standard stares of disbelief about her age, and she asked the Michigan investigators if she needed to review her resume' or could she continue? She laughed a little, so the Police Captain in charge of the Post said, "Thanks, Officer Trent. I'm sorry, but even though we were told about your youthful appearance, it was a bit shocking when you first walked in."

"I understand, Captain. I'm used to the stares, and I don't get upset by them. I just want you to know that I have a great deal of experience in this field and that I'm very good at what I do."

"Understood, Officer Trent. I thank you for your

cooperation in this investigation. I understand that you have tracked a sex-trafficking operation to the Flint area."

"I'm not sure that I tracked them here. In fact, I was abducted by a transporter during a sting operation in West Virginia. The transporter drugged me and delivered me to the Flint operator. I was lucky enough to overcome the first client the operator set me up to service, and I was able to escape."

"If you escaped in Flint, how did you end up in Bay City?" the captain asked.

"That's why I've asked that Steve Steiner be allowed to sit in on this meeting. From the sting in Kentucky last week, where I met Steve, I remembered that Steve lived in Cadillac. I contacted him and asked for help. I was trying to get away from the Flint area as soon as possible. Steve hired an Uber to take me to Bay City, where I stayed with a business associate of Steve's father."

"And why didn't you just call '911' and let the local police handle it?" the Chief asked.

"This Flint operator is a smooth character. He would have talked his way out of the situation. I want this guy charged with solid evidence, which he cannot squirm out of."

Then Steve interjected, "Captain, I think you need to be aware of Officer Trent's reputation in Kentucky, regarding sex trafficking. She is well respected in Louisville and elsewhere down there. I saw her arrange two sting operations in Kentucky recently with an entire operation shut down, the operators arrested, all necessary evidence gathered, and everyone involved remaining safe. I think she knows more about handling these crimes than you may realize."

"Understood, Officer Trent. What do you suggest? I think you may have more experience in this type of situation than we do."

"First of all, feel free to call me Liz. Next, our targets in Flint are Luke and Shauna. I don't know their last names. They have a small, 12-unit motel out near the truck assembly plant. I don't know the name of the motel, not seeing it except while I was drugged, but I can lead you to the Speedway station where I made my phone call. I saw the truck assembly plant when the Uber left the neighborhood."

"So then, we can just go down there and raid the motel," the captain said.

"Again, sir, this Luke character will just squirm out of any solid charges. I'm suggesting another sting, as we did in Kentucky, to let the guy talk his way into big trouble."

The captain was looking flustered, realizing that Liz was much more prepared than he expected, but he politely asked, "What do we need to do, Liz? Now I think I understand."

"I want to send in a customer, asking for a private session with a young girl. I'm certain that Shauna is Luke's 'house mother', keeping his stable of girls nearby. There is a long dark alley behind the motel, and I'd want good surveillance there, to see where the girl comes from, to meet the request. Once Luke sets him up in one of the motel rooms with the girl, then we raid the motel, as well as the house where the girls are kept."

"I certainly see why you're so highly regarded in Kentucky. I think we would have acted too quickly, and as you said, this Luke fella would skirt the charges. Who would you suggest as our fake client at the motel?"

There was a lot of discussion amongst the Troopers, and they thought they should call the Flint Post for suggestions.

"Can I offer to be the guy?" Steve offered. "I'm not a policeman, but I'm already familiar with how these stings work. I can ask the right questions and prompt this Luke fella to say things that will incriminate him. I'm going to testify in the Kentucky trials, so why not testify in Michigan?"

"I don't want you to put yourself in any danger, Steve," Liz said.

"What danger, Liz?" There is less risk here than I had in Kentucky. And while the raid is happening, I can try to get the girl to cooperate with us. I know how to do that as well."

"It's okay with me, as long as the Captain and our FBI Agents agree."

One of the FBI Agents spoke up, "From my experience, using a civilian as the lure for the perp, works better than using an Agent or a policeman. The civilian has just enough nervousness to be real, and the police officer comes across as too confident. If every-one agrees, I think we should accept Mr. Steiner's offer to pose as the customer."

Everyone seemed to agree, so the plans were set for late in the afternoon that same day. The surveil-lance positions would be set up beforehand, and Steve would enter the office once everyone was in position.

Liz rode with Steve on the way to Flint. Steve ran over the conversation he intended to use with Luke when he entered the motel office. Liz made a few suggestions, but said, "Are you sure you've never done this before? You sound much too convincing." Steve was worried, until he looked over at Liz, and saw the big grin on her face. Then it became very quiet, until Liz said, "I wanted you to be the one to do this, but I kept thinking about your mom. She already probably thinks I'm corrupting you, and after this, she may hate me."

"She'll interrogate you, for sure," Steve said. "But wait until you meet my mom. She sees through people's personalities and intentions like one of your investigators. Once she sees into your soul, she is going to love you."

Liz could tell that Steve almost continued to say, "like I love you," but she knew this was much too early in their unusual relationship to be talking about love and commitment. But she was happy to think that Steve was also thinking the same way.

"What are we going to do, Steve? How can we get

to know one another when our only dates involve sting operations or arresting people at a Gentlemen's Club?"

"I've been thinking the same thing. We certainly have had good opportunities to see each other's serious side, but we don't know a thing about the happier sides of our lives," Steve said.

"When this is over, would you be upset if this older woman suggested we have a real date?"

"I think I'd like that a lot," Steve said, and he reached over and squeezed Liz's hand.

It was decided that the Bay City Troopers would position themselves with Liz at the Speedway station. It wouldn't seem unusual for a bunch of officers to be meeting for coffee and donuts. The Flint Post Troopers would cover the alley behind the motel and watch for the girls who came to the motel. Once they saw the house where Shauna was getting the girls, they would notify Liz. Liz had set up Steve's cell phone to transmit a quick signal to her phone, once he was in the room with the girl. Then Liz and her group would raid the front of the motel.

Steve looked nervous when Liz stood at the door of his truck. "So, you have enough cash for this? I'll turn in a voucher if we can't get it returned today. That might be tough to do. You want to be a little nervous. Young guys are always nervous when asking for their first prostitute, aren't they? Oh, that's right, you said you've never done this," and she gave him a big smile. "You'll do fine, my man. And tonight, we'll laugh about it over dinner with Annette. Tomorrow, I get interrogated by your mom."

That brought a big smile to Steve's face, and he drove to the motel.

At the motel, Steve went into the office. The lights were on, but there was no one around. Steve saw the sign over the buzzer on the desk 'PUSH FOR SERVICE', and he pushed it. He heard voices in the back room, and then the door opened. At first, a woman's face looked through the door, but when she saw Steve, she said, "Luke, you have a customer."

Luke came out to the office and said, "You need a room for the night?"

Steve answered, "Well, the guys I worked with at the truck plant today said I might find a girl over here."

"What exactly are you looking for, young man?" Luke asked.

"I'm not real experienced, so I was hoping you maybe had a young girl who I could spend some time with?"

"What gave you the idea that you could find a girl here? This isn't a whorehouse, you know."

"Oh, I'm sorry," Steve said. "The guys at the plant told me that Luke could set me up. Maybe I came to the wrong place."

"Ahh, so the boys mentioned Luke? I normally don't do this kind of thing, but it seems like you've talked to some of my friends. Can't be too careful these days. I run a nice place. "Young girls who are willing can be hard to find. They cost a little more, you know. Just how much are you willing to spend?"

"I could spare about $300. Would that be enough?" Steve asked.

"Hey, you look like a real nice guy. If you promise to treat this sweet little girl real gentle, I can line you up for $400, and you can keep her for three hours. Deal?"

"Well, okay. Maybe I can work a couple extra days for more money."

"If you have the $400, I'll get you set up down in Room-6."

Steve gave Luke the money and Luke gave Steve the room keys. Then Luke went to the back door and yelled, "Shauna, would you please ask Tracy if she would like to spend a few hours with this nice young man? He's going to be gentle with her."

Then he turned back to Steve and told him Room 6 was about halfway to the end.

"Have a nice time. You'll really like Tracy. A real young girl for you."

Steve went to Room-6 and sat on the bed. A few minutes later, a girl walked in with a real look of fear on her face. "Hi. I'm Tracy," she said.

"How old are you, Tracy?" Steve asked her.

"I'm not sure if I'm supposed to say," Tracy said.

"I'm not here to hurt you" Steve assured her. "I'm here to help. How did you end up working for Luke?"

Steve opened his cell phone and pushed the button Liz had programmed as he listened to Tracy's responses.

"A lady found me on the street in Cleveland. My father would beat me when he got drunk, so I left home. The lady brought me here, and Luke is real nice to me."

"But Luke has you doing things with his customers?"

"Just for his friends, like you. I want to make Luke happy because he's so nice to me. He just asks me to be nice to his friends, and he always promises to have his friends treat me gentle. You'll be gentle, won't you?"

"Yes, but tell me how old you are?"

"I'll be fifteen next month. That's okay, isn't it? I want you to be happy."

Then Steve heard a lot of cars in the parking lot and looked out the window.

"Stay here, Tracy," he said. "I want to see what's going on."

He approached one of the Trooper's cars and asked the officer to keep an eye on Room-6, so Tracy wouldn't run away.

Steve then walked into the office where Luke was being confronted by the Bay City Captain. "I'm not sure what you're insinuating here. I run a decent little motel. I don't have any girls working for me."

"Hey, Luke, I just paid you $400 for Tracy down in Room-6," Steve said. "Tracy works for you, and I paid to have her for three hours. I want my money back."

"No, you paid me a little extra to look the other way. You said you'd picked up this young girl off the streets, and you wanted some time with her," Luke very coolly said. "I didn't like the idea, but I didn't want any trouble, so I agreed. She's your girl, not mine."

The office door opened and in walked Liz. Luke was visibly surprised and confused when he looked up and saw her.

"I should have that girl arrested," he said, after quickly collecting himself. "She came in here with a salesman a couple days ago, drugged the man, tied him to the bed, stole all his money, and then broke my window to sneak out the back."

The Bay City Captain turned to Liz and said, "Officer Trent, do you recognize this man?"

Liz said, "Hi, Luke. How's business? Got any new talent lately?"

"I have no idea who this woman is," Luke said.

"But you just told these officers that I hog-tied one of your customers."

"I must have been mistaken."

Steve whispered to Liz that he was going to bring Tracy to the office, and he stepped out. He went back to Room-6 and told Tracy that the police were there.

"Will I be arrested? I don't want to go back home. Is Luke okay? He promised to take care of me."

Steve said, "Can you come to the office and tell the police what you just told me?

"Will it help Luke? I need to be nice to Luke."

"I'm not sure if it will help, but there is a nice young lady there. Her name is Liz. She will help to keep you safe."

"Okay. I can come and see if I can help."

Steve took Tracy to the office and again, Luke looked a little scared. Tracy said, "Are you going to be okay, Luke? I tried to make your friend happy, but then the police came. You promised to take care of me. What's happening?" Luke was silent, staring at Tracy. Then Tracy realized things were not the same and she started to cry.

Liz put her arm around Tracy's shoulder and led her out the door. Steve followed and could hear Liz comforting Tracy. Tracy said, "I can't go home. My father hates me." Liz told her they could find a way to keep her safe, without sending her home. Then a Flint Post Trooper pulled into the parking lot. "Officer Trent? I think they need you in the alley. That lady who brought this girl around is holed up in a house back there with a bunch of girls."

Liz asked Tracy, "Does Shauna take care of you for Luke? How many other girls do you live with, Tracy?"

"Yes, Shauna is nice to us. There are four more girls. We live together and have fun."

"Tracy, would you stay here with Steve, please? I need to go and talk with Shauna."

"Sure. I'll stay here."

Liz hopped into the Trooper's squad, and they drove into the alley. Liz thought the alley didn't look much better in daylight than when she escaped, just the day before. The Trooper said, "At first, we thought there wasn't a house back here, with the girls you expected to find. But we saw the bleached blond, older woman you described, leading that teenager girl down the alley. We thought it was a mother with her little teen daughter. We couldn't believe how young that girl was. Then the woman came right back to the same house, so we figured it was the right place.

"You'll probably be surprised that some of the others are also just young teens. They have a tough life at home, find out it's not any better on the streets, and then they get into an operation like this. Some operators work with threats, drugs and beatings, but the smarter ones, like these two, use kindness and psychology to control their girls. They think that sexual favors for their 'friends' are a fair price for a warm place to stay and a full stomach. This Luke guy is a real pro at controlling these girls."

The house was surrounded by police squads. Shauna was refusing to open the door, and Liz went up on the back porch. Liz said, "Shauna, you may as well come out. You remember me? It was Sasha, the one who escaped the other night. My real name is Officer Elizabeth Trent. I'm a sex-crimes investigator with the Kentucky State Police. We've already arrested your supplier, Darla, down in West Virginia. We can wait until the search warrant arrives in an hour, but we're just going to sit here and wait. Tracy says you treat her and the girls well, so it sounds like you are just helping Luke. Why don't we just make this easy? Come out now and talk. Show some cooperation and things will be better for you."

There was a pause, and then Liz saw Shauna coming

to the door. She opened it and said, "My God, you're a cop? I really thought you were seventeen. What do you want?"

"I think you realize that I saw your whole operation, from Darla drugging me, transporting me, Luke grooming me for cooperation, setting me up with his client who liked Russian girls, and now this. The only thing I didn't experience was where you kept the other girls. So, you must realize that it's all over. Will you help us interview the girls, so we can figure out how to help them? Tracy says you treated them all well, and they trust you, but they will have to leave. Like Tracy, they don't want to go home, so I'll work with social services to take care of them."

"You'd do that? I didn't think that cops cared about these girls."

"I care, and I promise that I'll find a way to help them. I saw that you cared about these girls too. Maybe you came from a similar troubled home as these girls experienced. If so, I know the social services people would like you to work with them, and that way you can be sure these girls are well cared for. Would you be willing to do that? I could recommend that to the local authorities."

"Are you sure you're a real cop? You sure don't talk like one." Shauna said. "Alright, I'll introduce you."

"I could show you a badge," Liz said, "but the badge won't help these girls. You and I are concerned about their welfare and that's what counts."

After Shauna introduced Liz to the rest of the

girls, Liz returned to the motel where Steve was still talking with Tracy. Liz told Tracy she could return to Shauna's house and talk with the female officer who was talking with Shauna and the other girls.

"What's going to happen to her?" Steve asked after Tracy left. "She's had a tough life, and she feels more loved by Luke and Shauna than anyone else she's known in her life.

"That's the problem with operations like this one. That place the minister and the Donaldsons ran in Kentucky, used drugs and force to control the girls. They were happy to get free of them. Here, Luke and Shauna used caring and safety. For girls who may never have known that in their life, they did whatever they were asked to do, just to repay Luke's kindness. If that meant sex with his 'friends', then that was how they repaid his kindness. I experienced it, and because I wasn't the typical homeless girl, Luke tempted me with being his personal, live-in girl. Shauna played a good part in that ploy.

"The FBI and State guys are going to keep the girls at the house across the alley tonight, so they can interview the girls tomorrow. I'm going to call the local social services organizations to arrange places for them to stay and receive proper counseling. We can run up to Annette's place tonight, but I may need to come back to Flint tomorrow to help with that process. But before we leave, I have a debt to pay to that Speedway attendant. I hope the same guy is working tonight, the one who called your mom the other night."

Liz entered the Speedway and sure enough, the same guy was working. He immediately recognized her and said, "Are you safe tonight, or still in trouble?"

"I'm safe, thanks to you. And this is the fella we called in Cadillac."

Steve shook the fella's hand and said, "Thank you so much for believing her story, and letting her make that call."

"Like I told her, it was too crazy not to be true."

"Well, I'm here for two reasons," said Liz. "First, to tell you that you can now tell your friends what happened. It will probably be in the paper over the next few days. I know that the Bay City paper will have a special column, later in the week. But second, I'd like to invite you to lunch tomorrow, and I can give you the whole story like I promised."

"I'd really like that. Can I invite my girlfriend to come along? She'd love to meet you, I'm sure."

Liz's cell phone rang. "Captain Kelly. I'm glad you called. We just finished the raid in Flint, and all went well. Were you able to arrest Darla over in West Virginia?"

"We did. She won't talk. I'd like you to come down here as soon as possible, for two reasons. The first is for you to confront this Darla lady. Once she knows she kidnapped an officer, she may change her mind. However, the second reason may be bad. The team of FBI Agents and West Virginia Troopers who performed the search of the two locations found a shallow grave out back of that old farmhouse. The body they found was a young girl. We aren't sure yet, but we think she matches the description of Leslie's sister."

"Oh, God. I was afraid of that. None of the girls here in Flint matched her description. Are you going to have an autopsy performed?"

"Yes. That's being done first thing in the morning."

"Captain Kelly, can I ask you not to tell Leslie until I arrive? I'm the one that told her we'd find her sister, so I think I need to be the one to break the news if the body is in fact her sister."

"I understand. We can wait."

"I'll drive down tomorrow, arriving late. I'll see you in your office the next morning and we can decide on what needs to be done."

"Thank you, Liz. I know this search for her was personal for you. It's not looking like a happy ending."

Steve said, "Leslie's sister? It sounded bad from what I could hear."

"The identification is not final, but it appears to be her. Let's head to Annette's. I need a glass of wine. And I'll overlook this under-age guy having one with me if he chooses."

"I thought you said my age didn't matter?"

"Well, I'm a cop after all, and you're still a month or so away from being twenty-one. But seeing you frequent Gentlemen's Clubs and brothels, I guess I also need to overlook a glass of wine."

"Using my mom's words, you're getting awfully snarky!" And by the way, I will be twenty-one in just three weeks."

Chapter 17

THE STORY

Annette and the three kids were all excited to have overnight guests again. Annette had talked to Stormi that afternoon. She had delivered the new tug and barges to Traverse City, because of Ashley and Adam's kidnapping, and she was on her way home. Liz would get a chance to meet Stormi at breakfast before she and Steve headed back to Flint.

Annette was very interested in how the girls, who were victims of sex trafficking, were to be treated and started asking Liz questions, so she could include her answers in the column she was writing.

Liz started, "The one sure thing is that we cannot just send them home. The young girl who Luke sent to Steve's room today, was only fourteen but told Steve she was fifteen. Her father had been beating her when he got drunk, so she left home. If we sent her back, she'd be back on the streets in no time, if her father didn't kill her beforehand. There is a U.S. Department of Health and Human Services program, called the

Trafficking Victims Protection Act, but hey, it's the Federal Government. They put it all on paper, but somebody has to make it happen. I called the National Human Trafficking Hotline on our drive this after-noon, and they put me in touch with three Michigan-based organizations that specialize in getting these girls back to a normal, safe life. At least more normal than what they've been experiencing. That guy in Flint treated them well, probably better than their families had, but they had to keep his friends happy. Keeping them happy included sex, probably several times a day. The police confiscated over $12,000 in cash in Luke's back room. Steve had paid $400 for three hours with a fourteen-year-old girl, who Steve said was just plain scared. Lucrative business."

"So, what comes next?" Annette asked.

"The Michigan Division of Victim Services will have several representatives at the house tomorrow. They'll find jobs and training for those girls over eighteen, as well as counseling. They will also locate foster homes for the younger ones. There'll also be investigations done on their families, to see why the girls left home. If it was sexual or physical abuse, the girls will need additional counseling for mental issues."

"It's hard to believe, and I'm sure this is just the tip of the iceberg, isn't it, Liz?"

"I heard of a case in Georgia where they had over 150-victims found in just one raid, and well over a hundred arrests of those who held them captive, trans-porters, and so on. This Flint operation was a small one, with five trafficked girls and only two arrests. I'm sure there are others in the area, so I'm hoping that the FBI and State Police have now become more aware, due to this experience. But tomorrow, Steve and I are headed to West Virginia. They found a body at the drop-off location where I was first taken and drugged. We suspect it was the young sister of one of the girls we set free in the Louisville area. If it does turn out to be her sister, I want to be there to break the news."

"I'll be honest, Liz. I couldn't do your job. It's hard enough just writing about it, no less living it every day like you have to do."

"I've been discussing that with Steve. I'm feeling a burn-out coming. I know I take my job too personally, and it wears on me. I've decided to go to Law School and become a prosecutor. I can stop wearing dirty, pissy clothes and use the court system to put these monsters in prison. Once these current cases are completed, I'll make the jump. I know my parents will be happy, but they might object to my decision to attend the U of M, here in Ann Arbor, instead of Kentucky."

"Any good reasons to pick Michigan? Doesn't Kentucky have a good Law School?"

"It'll just be nice to start school with a built-in good friend, I guess," Liz answered.

"I can't argue with that. It seems like you two are good for one another," Annette said.

"My only worry is explaining all of this to Mrs. Steiner. What will she think?"

"You'll love Lois. Give her time to get to know you.

She's pretty protective of Steve but just explain your intentions. She'll listen and evaluate you for a while. If you mean well, she'll come around."

"Can I ask a favor, Annette? I promise to help you write this story for your paper, but can you wait to release it until I come back? I want you to get the whole story, and there are too many open ends right now. I'm going to ask the Michigan State Police to keep this bust under wraps until I get back from West Virginia because the two cases are inter-related. After I wrap up the Flint case and the one in West Virginia, I promised Steve we'd go to meet his mother. After that, I'll spend a couple days with you and help you write your column. I know you cannot control the news in the other papers, but if you can tell them to hold off, tell them you'll be getting a real scoop by the end of the week."

"The editors at the other papers trust me, so if I ask them to hold off, I think they will. That may not work with the TV stations, but I'll try."

"Thanks, Annette. I hate the flashy stories on the news, 'Local Brothel Raided', but they miss the real meat of the story, dealing with Human Trafficking, which is the real problem."

The next morning, as promised, the other half of the couple was home. Steve's father, Curt, had been looking to hire a new captain ten years ago, for the expanding Strauss Marine Construction Company. He interviewed Stormi Weaver and watched her in operation. She had come highly recommended, even by her competition for the job, and Curt recommended that Bill Strauss should hire Stormi. Now that Curt's time was taken up by management duties, Stormi was the Senior captain in the fleet of tugs, now numbering fourteen.

Steve awoke on the sofa, hearing Stormi in the process of brewing a pot of coffee. He snuck up behind her and hugged her. "Just so you know, hotshot, I heard you coming. Good thing too, or I'd have you cleaning up the floor, you little shit! Although you aren't as little as when I first met you. How's school? This is your last year, right?"

"Yeah, last year, unless I stay to get my Master's degree."

"The need for a Master's wouldn't have anything to do with a Law Student I heard about?"

"Don't give him any ideas," Liz yelled from the top of the stairs. "This is the first I've heard of that idea. I'm already in trouble with his mother, and now he wants to make it worse?" Liz came down the stairs and shook Stormi's hand. Stormi then grabbed Liz for a hug and said, "We give hugs in the Strauss Marine family."

"It's great to meet you, Stormi. I heard Curt and Steve mention your name down in Kentucky last week. All good, by the way."

"I don't envy you meeting Lois though. First, you take Steve and Curt to a Gentlemen's Club, and now I hear you set Steve up with a girl at a brothel. Great introduction to Mrs. Steiner."

"Trust me. I'm scared to death about it. May be good that I have another couple days to think over this meeting."

"Lois can be tough, but you'll be fine, I think," and Stormi cackled, so Liz questioned the answer.

"Darn it, Stormi. Don't scare her. She is concerned enough on her own," Annette yelled.

"Where's the tribe? I nearly have breakfast ready," Stormi asked.

"I told them to stay in their rooms this morning. They woke up Steve and Liz with their chatter yesterday. I'll tell them they can come down now," Annette answered.

"I understand you have a terrible reason for your trip today. One of the girls was found dead?" Stormi asked.

"We're pretty sure it's the fourteen-year-old sister of one of the girls that Steve and I helped last week. They should have a positive ID by the time we get there. Probably killed by the same woman who transported me. If so, she'll be up on murder charges, as well as sex trafficking."

Chapter 18

SAD ROAD TRIP

After breakfast and saying their goodbyes, Liz and Steve packed up and hit the road. Steve started driving so that Liz could get on the phone. She called Captain Kelly and he confirmed that the body was definitely identified as Leslie's sister. "Any word yet on the autopsy?" Liz asked. Kelly said not yet, so Liz said, "Please call me when you get the results. I have a suspicion about what they'll find."

They stopped to see how things were going in Flint. Liz took contact information for all of the social services women who were working with the girls. Then Liz gave each of the five girls a hug and promised to follow their progress.

"One last thing, Steve. Let's call the Speedway guy, grab an early lunch, and then hit the road."

"I think he'd understand if you put off the lunch date, Liz."

"No. That guy trusted me and got me out of danger. He may not know how important that was, but I know. It's a debt I have to repay. It's not the lunch but showing him that he was important."

"I understand. And again, you impress me with your caring."

After lunch, they headed to Ashland. Liz asked Steve to stop at the same rest stop near Ann Arbor, where Darla had stopped on the way north. "It was over there, on the other side of the highway. She had cut me back to only a quarter dose of that drug that she kept pumping into my butt, but I still could barely stand up. I won't be able to find the other place she stopped, somewhere in Ohio, but she damn near had to carry me into the toilet. Whatever that stuff was, it was super strong."

"I can hear how upset you are about her drugging you. I guess you can't wait to confront her?"

"You've got that right. I think I came close to dying that first night. I pride myself for not ever having taken drugs, and then this woman starts injecting me, having no knowledge of dosages. I think that young girl died of a drug overdose, given by Darla."

"Wow. You really suspect that?" Steve asked.

"I'd bet on it. Probably the same thing she gave me."

Now Liz was driving, and Steve was checking in with his dad, who just got home from the hospital. Steve gave Curt a short synopsis of yesterday's events and told Curt, "Dad, Liz wants to drive me home when this is over, so she can meet Mom. Will you please prepare Mom? I'm thinking Liz is a bit scared of what Mom thinks of her." There was a pause, then Steve said, "No, don't tell her that. Be serious. Hey Dad, Liz's phone is ringing, so I'd better get off. See you in a few days. Love you too."

Liz pulled over on the shoulder and answered her phone. She told Steve he could drive, but Steve said he wanted to listen to the conversation.

"Yes, Captain Kelly. We've stopped. Go ahead."

"Liz, you probably won't be surprised by this, but the girl died from a drug overdose. The Medical Examiner said she also had numerous bruises, consistent with maybe a fall down those stairs, but the girl had been injected with an animal tranquilizer. Something called Xylazine. He said the dose was strong enough to have dropped a good size, thousand-pound horse. For a girl weighing under 100-pounds, she had no chance to survive. Do you think that's what she injected you with, Liz?"

"She must have reduced the dose on me, but it knocked me out for what I guessed was twelve hours. She then cut that dose in half, and I slept a few more hours. Finally, she only used a quarter dose on me. Can we charge Darla with murdering Leslie's sister? She certainly deserves it."

"We'll see what the prosecutor says. I sure hope so, but because it wasn't premeditated, it may get dropped to manslaughter."

"Does Darla know about me yet? I want to see her face when she realizes she kidnapped a State Trooper."

"No, we saved that pleasure for you, Officer Trent.

I'll see you in the morning, and we'll go over to Huntington. Have a safe drive."

"So, your hunch was right?" Steve said.

"Yes, and this is why I want to become a prosecutor. This woman deserves a murder charge, not manslaughter."

The rest of the drive was pretty quiet. Steve could see that Liz was upset and deep in thought. He felt it was best to leave her alone.

That night, Liz checked them into a small hotel near the Kentucky State Police Post in Ashland. Steve was surprised when Liz asked for adjoining rooms. They went to dinner and then they each went to their own room. Not much was said during dinner, and Steve could feel Liz's depression. She was taking this death very personally.

Steve was sitting in bed, checking his emails when he heard a knock on the adjoining door. He opened it and Liz stood there, in Steve's mom's baggy T-shirt, obviously crying. "Don't get the wrong idea, okay. I just need a good hug." Steve gave her a long hug and stroked her hair. Liz suddenly pulled away and looked at him. She gave him the most passionate kiss he had ever received in his young life. Then Liz said, "Thank you. Now go to bed. I set my alarm for six."

The following morning, Liz seemed refreshed when they went to breakfast. Steve had hardly slept. Liz kept staring into Steve's eyes but said nothing. Finally, Liz said, "I extended our rooms for another night, and then we can drive back to Michigan tomorrow. Can we get to Cadillac in one day?"

"About nine hours, so I guess," Steve said.

"Okay. Is there a hotel near your parent's home? I'll make a reservation for myself."

"Mom will want you to stay with us, I think."

"Let's talk to her later today. See what she thinks."

They went to the Ashland State Police Post in Kentucky. Captain Kelly looked nervously at Liz, and then he asked, "Would you mind if I hug you? We darn near got you killed. We were sloppy. I'm so sorry."

Liz answered his question by reaching up to Kelly's six-three frame and starting the hug herself. Steve could see the emotion on Captain Kelly's face. He had obviously been very concerned about Liz's welfare. Several other Troopers came into Kelly's office, and although no further hugs were exchanged, Steve saw the relieved smiles on the men's faces. They hadn't worked together very long, but they were a brotherhood, and they almost lost a sister.

After the polite chit-chat died down, Liz said, "So, you have the guy from Independence who trafficked Leslie and her sister. Can we tie him to this delivery and the murder?"

"We'll be lucky to get murder charges to stick on Darla, but we'll try."

"Hell, her smaller dose darn near killed me. No wonder that poor girl died."

"Let's work on Darla. She's singing a tune about

helping wayward girls back to Jesus. I can't wait to see what she says when you walk into the interrogation."

"Does she know that you've found the body?"

"No. We've saved that for you to tell her. We figured it might tie in well with the shock of seeing you walk in."

"Thanks for that," Liz said.

Chapter 19

CONFRONTATION

Liz rode with Steve, following Captain Kelly and one of his investigators over the border to Huntington. Huntington was a nice river town with a colorful history, but river towns are also known for their toughness. Darla, full name Darla McKinney, was being held in the Federal Building in downtown Huntington. Liz watched the interrogation through the two-way mirror, and she saw that Darla certainly had her act prepared.

"Gentlemen, I don't know what you're talking about. Ask any of my neighbors, and they'll tell you that I am a service to the community. I find all these liquored-up young women and I rescue them off the streets. I sober them up, save them in Jesus' name, and return them to good lives, with good jobs. How can you accuse me of dealing in this crime, some kind of traffic?"

Liz thought it was time to change the tactics. She entered the interrogation room and stayed silent as she sat across the table from Darla. She saw the fear in Darla's eyes, but Darla stayed quiet. The interrogator then asked, "You are telling me that you did not drive to Michigan last week? Is that true?"

"I may have driven over the bridge into Ohio, but why would I go to Michigan?" Darla tried to avoid Liz's eyes, but she saw Liz staring at her, but remaining quiet.

"Do you know a man, Luke Yaeger, who owns a motel in Flint Michigan?"

"How would I know anyone in Flint, Michigan?" Darla replied.

"We have a witness who saw you at that motel, calling Mr. Yaeger by name."

"What witness?" Darla asked.

Liz just raised her hand and said, "Me, Darla. Remember me?"

"I think this is one of those fallen girls I tried to save for Jesus. She must have fallen back into temptation. I think I remember her from some time back."

"Darla, give it up. My name is Elizabeth Trent. I'm a sex-trafficking investigator with the Kentucky State Police. A guy named Oscar dropped me off at your farmhouse early this week. You injected me with a nearly lethal dose of Xylazine. Then you continued to inject me during our long drive to Flint. I heard you tell Luke to pay you in the normal way, so I assume that the subpoena to seize your documents and bank accounts will show that payment. Luke and Shauna are in custody, those girls who you transported up there will also testify against you."

Darla was finally silent, and then she said, "I can't believe that you're a cop. How could Oscar have done this to me?"

"Same as the rest of you, Darla. He'd do anything to save his own ass or shorten his sentence. But tell me, Darla. Where do you get that animal tranquilizer? You know, you damn near killed me with that first overdose? Give us your source and show some co-operation. It might help you."

"Doc Nooley in town. He thinks I keep horses at the farm. But I lightened up on you when I saw it knocked you out. You were okay."

"Maybe I survived, but what about that fifteen-year-old from Independence? How much did you give her?"

"I don't know what you're talking about? Really."

"Oh, sure you do, Darla. You know, the little 90-pound blond girl. The one we found buried behind your farmhouse. Here she is in this picture from her sister, and then here she is in the grave behind your house, and here she is on the autopsy table. How much did you give her?"

"Oh, that sweet little thing. One of those I rescued. She was drunk and fell down the stairs, and she died. She had no family, so I had to bury her."

"Not even close, Darla. Here's a copy of the autopsy report. Death due to lethal dose of Xylazine. The bruises on her body didn't cause her death. You killed her with an overdose of that tranquilizer. Was she trying to run away? Why did you need to tranquilize her? She was only fifteen, and you took her life away from her. I wish West Virginia had a death penalty. Lethal Injection would be great for you. But I guess life in prison will have to be enough. I'll see you at your trial, Darla. I have a lot of first-hand experience to share with the jury." And with that, Liz got up and walked out of the room, and Darla refused to talk any further.

Liz came out and found Steve in his truck. He saw the look on Liz's face and saw the hate in her eyes. "You saw her? What happened?" he asked.

"If she gets off, don't let me near a gun. Okay?'

"Trust me. I won't."

"Let's head to Independence. I need to tell Leslie."

"Give me the address for the GPS."

"Here. And we're staying at a hotel tonight. I need another one of those hugs if you promise not to kiss me, like last night."

"But you're the one who kissed me!" Steve said.

"But you didn't stop me. So, this time, stop me!"

Steve was starting to see that Liz was a very complicated woman.

The GPS guided them to a small duplex in Independence, Kentucky. Steve asked if he should go in with Liz, but she said it needed to be done alone. She said it may take a while, so relax.

Liz went to the door and rang the bell. Leslie came to the door with a smile, but then saw Liz's grim face.

"You found Linda, and it's not good. I just knew it would be bad. She was so young. This is just so wrong."

The two women went inside and cried together. Few words were said because there was nothing left to say. As Liz was about to leave, she said, "Be sure to show up every time your transporter appears in a courtroom. Let the prosecutor know you're there and sit up front where the judge can see you. It helps. They might hate these guys, but you have to remind them why. Be available to testify against him, both in your case and for your sister."

They hugged long at the door when Liz said her final goodbye. Then Liz got in the truck and said to Steve, "Can we stop in Ann Arbor for the night? I want to see the U of M campus. I'll look for a hotel near there."

That night, Liz again booked adjoining rooms. She needed her hug, then went back to her room and Steve heard her crying for a long time. Then he heard another knock on the door. Liz said, "I need another one of those hugs, so I can sleep. If I try to kiss you, push me back into my room."

"What's your aversion to kissing?" Steve asked.

"Then I may not want to stop. I'm afraid to ruin what we have. It's too early for that."

This hug lasted nearly a half-hour. Liz wasn't crying this time, and Steve tried to talk to her. Liz put her finger on Steve's lips to stop him from talking, sat on Steve's lap, and she buried her face in his neck. She kept nuzzling Steve's neck and occasionally sighed. Then Liz got up, said thank you with the most loving look Steve had ever seen and went back to her room where she slept well. Again, Steve barely slept, and he knew that life with Liz might be very complicated, but exciting.

The next day, they drove around the U of M campus and Liz saw the Law School. Liz had the most contented look on her face, it made Steve happy for her. This was the most relaxed he had seen her over their tumultuous two weeks together. Later, they headed north towards Cadillac.

Chapter 20

ANOTHER MISSING PERSON?

Steve pulled into his family's driveway in Cadillac. His twin siblings, Robert and Ellen, now age-10, ran out to greet him. Steve had been very close to his little brother and sister since they were born, and Lois and Curt even allowed him to choose their names. It was ten o'clock at night and Steve said, "Hey you guys, it's way past your bedtime. What are you doing up so late?"

"Mom said we could stay up to see you when you got home if we promised to sleep late tomorrow morning. She said she wanted to keep you two up late tonight for a long talk. Are you in trouble, Steve?" Ellen asked.

"No, I think it's Liz who's in trouble," Steve said with a chuckle. "So Liz, this is Ellen and the quiet one is Robert. They're about to start 3rd grade this fall. I got to hold them the day they were born, and they were nice then, but they've gotten to be real snotty since then." Both of the young ones gave Steve a weird look but grinned at him.

Liz liked the easy banter that Steve had with his little sister and brother. There was obvious caring between them. But Steve's off-hand remark about her being the one in trouble didn't help any to settle her nerves.

"Come on you guys, why don't you take Liz in the house. She just can't wait to see Mom and Dad." With that remark, Liz gave Steve a pretty hard smack on his upper arm. Enough that Steve grabbed and rubbed his arm.

When they entered the house, Ellen said, "Look who's here Mom. Steve finally came home."

Curt quickly got up from the sofa and came across to the entry hall. He avoided Steve and went directly to Liz, first grabbing her hand, with a big smile, and then giving her a huge hug. "I hear that our adventure in Kentucky was just a warm-up for you. This terrible situation in Michigan made the Kentucky deal look like nothing."

"Great to see you again, Mr. Steiner. I must admit, the trip to Michigan scared me half to death, and my final escape was pretty unnerving too. This operation made Louisville look like nothing, I'm afraid."

"Annette told me about the column she's putting

together for the Bay City paper. She's waiting for you to help her finish it, and she said the local TV station wants to interview you for a story. I would say you were in a terrible situation. The drugging and captivity she described seemed lucky for you to survive."

"You may not have heard, but the girl, Leslie, who was one of the girls we rescued in Kentucky, also had a young sister who disappeared. We believe she was destined for the Flint operation as well. The same woman who drugged me and drove me to Flint drugged Leslie's sister, and the sister died. They found her body buried behind the house those people used for a drop-off location, the one where I was originally taken."

"Oh, my. I remember Leslie. She was the one that ran away from the hotel," Curt said. "But I'd better quit talking and introduce you to Lois. Steve's probably warned you, she's ready for an inquisition."

"Knock it off, Curt," Lois said. "I've heard enough of the story from you and Steve, so I finally figured out what was going on. But I do want to learn a little more about Liz."

"That alone should scare you, Liz. Any female who comes close to our son receives a third-degree interrogation. Even poor little Becky, back in Middle School, dared to kiss Steve on the cheek, and Lois made me warn Steve about wily women," Curt said.

"Oh, come on. I wasn't that bad," Lois complained.

"I don't know, Mom," Steve said. "I remember that

conversation with Dad. He said it was okay if Becky just kissed me on the cheek, but I was not allowed to kiss her back."

Liz saw that the chatter was good-natured, but Lois was becoming quite embarrassed. It was nice to see the good-natured, yet serious interactions in this family, who loved and respected one another.

Lois said, "I think we need a glass of wine to lighten this mood a little. Annette said you enjoy a good white wine. Is that right, Liz?"

"I like red or white. And yes, I think I need a glass. Steve has been warning me all day that I was in big trouble." With that, Steve gave a real guilty grimace.

"Steven! You didn't. I told you to tell Liz that I'd moved beyond that mood. As you can imagine, Liz, these two purposely only gave me part of the story, knowing I would wonder just what the heck was going on. You can imagine what I thought when Curt told me he and Steve were in a Gentleman's Club. I know and trust them both, but they purposely only gave me part of the story until later. Well, luckily before this bordello story hits the news, Annette called me to explain what was going on. When will that hit the news? At least Annette understood what Steve was doing was part of your raid plans, and Steve was in no actual danger. But let's relax, so we can talk. In fact, I think Curt and Steve should disappear for a while and let the two of us chat."

A one-on-one chat with Steve's mom didn't exactly sound relaxing, but Liz knew she was the one who asked for this, so she couldn't object. "That sounds great," Liz said.

Steve joined the twins in the Family Room and Lois poured Liz a glass of wine. Curt stayed with Lois and Liz, but he knew this was not his time to talk, so he sat across from the two women.

Lois sat on the edge of the sofa and got right to the point, "Liz, you're a beautiful woman, and I can see why Steve is attracted to you. But I understand you are six years older than Steve, and I'm worried. Steve has been exposed to a lot of real-life at a young age, so I know he's not naïve. But with all you have been exposed to in your line of work, I worry about your influence on Steve. Do you understand my concern?"

"Mrs. Steiner, I do understand. Just so you know, I've told Steve, we are currently just good friends. I'm not ready for a serious relationship right now, and I understand your concern about Steve. However, please don't think that my exposure to illegal sex trafficking has made me experienced sexually, or a wanton woman. If anything, my experiences have made me apprehensive of sexual relationships."

"I didn't mean to imply..." Lois began.

"Please. Let me finish before I lose my nerve," Liz said. "I don't want to be rude, but I need to get this off my chest. I've been worried about this meeting for almost two weeks now.

Lois nodded and sat back.

"You see, I get ogled by a lot of men in my life because I look so young. Those men are not all bad people, but I know when the ogling is sexual. When Steve looked at me during our first meeting, I saw respect in his eyes even though he may have enjoyed my good looks. When I called him out publicly, I saw something different. His embarrassment showed that his parents had taught him respect, and watching him with Curt over those few days, I could tell that Steve was someone special. And just remember, I thought Steve looked to be in his mid-twenties at that first meeting. I didn't find out he was twenty until the following day when I had both Steve's and Curt's backgrounds checked out."

Curt jumped in, "Really? I didn't know that happened."

"Sure thing, Curt. You were becoming part of police action. It had to be done."

"Okay, but..." Lois tried to interrupt.

"I'm almost done, Mrs. Steiner. Can I please finish? Then I'd love to answer your concerns."

"I guess that's only fair, seeing I've put you in the hot seat. Go ahead, Liz."

"The six years difference between Steve and myself might matter if I was pushing for a serious relationship right now. I'm more scared about that than Steve may be, and probably more than you. Because of my job, men are not very interested in a relationship with me, and therefore, I have had zero serious relationships. Zero! I seldom get beyond a couple dates and the guys disappear. That hasn't scared Steve, which does make me wonder about him," Liz said, glancing into the next room at Steve. "He's seen me at my worst and has come to my aid when I was in trouble. I'm just asking you to trust me and understand that I want to get to know Steve better. If it becomes serious, I'll be sure to let you know. Okay, I'm done. Sorry for not letting you speak."

"Wow! I can see why Steve and Curt are impressed by you. I thought I'd have a lot to say, but you answered most of my questions better than if I had asked. However…"

"Okay, Liz. I knew she wasn't letting you off that easy," Curt said.

"Curt quit scaring this poor girl. Go join Steve and the twins. Let me talk to Liz alone."

Curt got up and left, smiling at Liz as he left.

"I like you, Liz. A lot! But my big question is, what has attracted you to Steve? I can see why Steve is smitten, but what really attracted you to Steve?"

"His blush."

"What do you mean?" Lois asked, looking very puzzled.

"Mrs. Steiner, I'm not conceited, but my mother told me I was cursed with good looks. I don't see it in myself, but I do get stares, which make me uncomfortable. The way I react is to call out the guy to embarrass him. I saw Steve looking at me and I embarrassed him. He blushed."

"I still don't fully understand, I guess. Why was blushing a big thing? Isn't that normal?"

"You see, that's normal because you raised Steve

to respect a woman. The 'bad boys' don't blush. They have a snappy comeback so that they don't lose face. But because you raised Steve to respect a woman, he was ashamed that he had made me feel uncomfortable, and he blushed."

"Now I understand. I know the look on those bad boys, as you call them. If I'd ever seen that look on Steve's face, I'd have smacked him."

"So, do you see? It's your fault that I'm attracted to Steve, Mrs. Steiner."

"Well, first of all, please call me Lois, now that we're friends. I know that Steve has not been happy with the girls his age who flirt with him. He's a serious young man, and I think he's been looking for a serious woman. If that turns out to be you, I'll be very happy.

"I have been so afraid of meeting you, Lois. I'm just glad this is over."

"The inquisition is over, Lois said, calling out to Curt and Steve. "You two can come back. And Ellen and Robert, you two get ready for bed."

Both Curt and Steve walked in with a little bit of worry on their faces.

"Did she tear you apart? She can be unmerciful sometimes," Steve asked.

"Not at all," Liz said. "She actually gave me some ammunition to keep you two guys in line. Thanks for that, Lois."

Lois smiled and winked at Liz, "I'll get the two kiddos in bed, and Curt, please refill our wine glasses while I'm gone."

After Liz left the room, Steve turned to Liz and said, "While you two were talking, Dad was updating me on local news.". "Before meeting you, and knowing about your work, this one bit of news wouldn't have sounded so serious. If you remember from earlier, we spoke about the little girl, Becky, from back in Middle School?"

"Sure, I remember. The one who kissed your cheek? Probably your first real girlfriend?"

"Well, she thought we were a thing until she saw me talking to other girls in high school. She was very possessive, and we parted ways. Becky comes from a family of seven kids. She was in the middle. Dad just told me that Becky's youngest brother, we think he's thirteen, is missing. It just happened yesterday. Knowing what I've learned lately, this news worries me. What do you think?"

"Can you call them now? I know it's late, but time is important. Find out if the boy has come home yet," Liz said. And Steve could tell that Liz was very concerned, even though she had minimal information.

"Sure, I can call. I'll do it now," Steve said.

While Liz and Curt chatted about the week's events, Steve got on the phone. He only had Becky's phone number recorded, so she answered, "I haven't heard from you since graduation. What's up, Steve?"

"Becky, my dad just told me your youngest brother is missing, I think it's Terry, right? Have you found him yet?"

"No. It'll be two days tomorrow and my folks are now frantic. They've called all his friends, and nobody has seen him. He'll probably show up. He probably stayed with a friend and forgot to call. He can take care of himself."

"Two weeks ago, I might have agreed, Becky. But my dad and I have met a woman who specializes in missing children. I'm going to ask her opinion, okay?"

Steve thought, *her brother may be okay, but I just can't ignore the possibility that some human trafficker is involved. From what I've learned the last couple weeks, I have to say something.*

"He's just missing. Are you referring to trafficking, like for sex? He's a boy, for crying out loud. Sex trafficking is what they warn girls about, not boys. And this is northern Michigan, not Detroit."

"I know what you think, Becky. But this woman is our house guest tonight. Can we come over and let her talk to your parents? You said they were concerned, so they may need to listen to her."

Lois walked into the Family Room to find Curt, Liz and Steve talking. They all looked worried, so Lois asked what was going on.

"Liz is worried about Becky Lilliquist's brother," Curt told her. "He's not come home for nearly two days now, and with what both Steve and I have learned over the last couple weeks, we think we should offer our help. At least we need to talk to Becky's parents about the possible consequences, and that they shouldn't wait any longer to ask for help."

"So, do you agree, Liz?" Lois asked.

"Oh, yes. Boys at age 13 are prime targets for traffickers. If we're wrong and he returns home, fantastic. But waiting another day, even hours, reduces the possibility of finding him if a trafficker has grabbed him."

"Then yes, let's call the Lilliquists. From what you three have told me, it would be foolhardy to wait, even until morning."

"I only have Becky's number in my phone, Mom. Do you have one of her parents' numbers?" Steve asked.

"Yes, I have Joan's number. Let me call her," said Lois.

Liz shared her ideas with Curt and Steve while Lois made her call. They overheard Lois's side of the conversation and determined that Mrs. Lilliquist's reaction had changed from skepticism to a willingness to talk with someone, whom Lois referred to as an expert in these matters. They also realized that Lois was purposely avoiding references to sex trafficking, so she wouldn't upset Joan Lilliquist any further than she already was.

Lois came back to the three and said, "We definitely need to get over there and help them. I'll let Joan explain the circumstances, but I think something bad has happened. One of us needs to stay home with the twins. Obviously, Liz and Steve should go over, and either Curt or I should probably go. Who would you think, Liz?"

"I think Steve has seen as much, even more than Curt, about the way these operations work, so Steve can cover the first-hand experience issues. So, if you wouldn't mind, I think Mrs. Steiner should come along. I think that your new understanding of this trafficking problem would be good for the parents to hear. Sometimes, hearing only from so-called experts can create an atmosphere of disbelief, because the parents may think the experts are seeing potential problems lurking behind every turn. If Lois can say things like, 'That's the way I used to think until Curt's captain was kidnapped', and other things she imagined couldn't happen, it may help Becky's parents to take this more seriously."

"Okay. That's settled, so we'd better get over there. Curt, you're the designated babysitter."

"Fine. I agree that Lois would be best for this situation."

The Lilliquists were waiting for them, eager to hear what they had to offer. There were the typical stares of disbelief when Liz was introduced, but Lois did a better job of touting Liz's qualifications than Liz could have done herself. Liz asked the boy's parents to tell them how and when the boy disappeared, and Tom Lilliquist started.

"Terry was playing and apparently getting good at baseball this summer. He told us he was accepted for a traveling team, playing other teams in Central Michigan. He said they were going to play a team in Ludington and Terry left on Thursday morning for the game and said he'd be back before dinner. When he didn't return, we didn't get worried until around nine that night. Then we tried to find Mr. Hanson, who Terry had told us was the manager of the team. The recreation center told us they didn't have anyone named Hanson on their staff, and that Terry had not been chosen for the traveling team."

"Have you spoken to any of the other boys on the baseball team, or staff at the recreation center? Particularly asking about the man Terry was with?" Liz asked.

"No, we haven't," said Mr. Lilliquist. "I think we thought things like this never happened in northern Michigan."

"If you know any of the other baseball players, I'd suggest calling them. Maybe their sons saw Terry talking with this man, and the boys could describe him."

"We'll start making those calls in the morning," said Mrs. Lilliquist.

"No, I'm sorry Joan," said Liz. "I think you need to start realizing that Terry has been kidnapped. Even if you wake up these parents, just tell them this has become serious, and you now realize that Terry has been abducted, and the police are involved."

"But the police aren't involved yet," Joan said. "You can't declare a person to be missing until after 24-hours."

"That missing person, 24-hour time is a myth, particularly for children. And Joan, I am a policewoman. I'm also a sex-crimes investigator with the Kentucky State Police. I've been working this week with the

Michigan State Police and the FBI, concerning sex-trafficking rings in Michigan. I fear that Terry may have been taken by one of these people. Please, call those parents now. Reaction time is important, and he's already been gone overnight."

The parents appeared to be in shock, so Lois got them to put together a list of Terry's friends and classmates, and they started calling. They asked the parents to wake their son, if necessary, to see if they remembered any older people hanging with Terry at the baseball park. Two of the boys remembered someone. They had felt sorry about Terry not being picked for their traveling team, and this man had told Terry he was starting another team.

In the meantime, Liz called the local Cadillac State Police Post, introduced herself, and explained her role in the recent Flint trafficking case. The Trooper on the phone said he'd heard about the Flint raid and would call his supervisor, as well as the Flint and Bay City Posts, to notify them of this potential, new abduction.

Within fifteen minutes, the Flint Post Captain called Liz. "Officer Trent. I'm glad you called. I didn't think this would involve you, but somehow you always seem to be drawn to these cases. Since we made the arrests of Luke and Shauna at that motel, we've had an undercover officer running the motel, in case we might find any further illegal activities. We've left Luke's voicemail message active, thinking our officer's voice might spook the callers. Early yesterday morning, there was an unusual message from a man who was trying to limit the details of his message, but he said, and I'll paraphrase, 'I found that young male you needed. Want to deliver soon. Call me. Tinker.' Until my desk guy told me about your call, we weren't sure what it meant. I might be the boy you're looking for."

"While I was locked in Luke's backroom, I remember overhearing Luke talking to a caller, who wanted to have a young boy for the evening. Luke said he'd have one for the next time the guy was in town. I'm sure if anyone but Luke calls this Tinker guy, he'll spook. Let me ask you, what is the status of the charges against Luke? Do you think he'd cooperate and call Tinker, to make the delivery?"

"Shauna has opened up to us, but Luke is not co-operating. Do you think if Shauna made the call, this Tinker guy would recognize her? I just hope Tinker hasn't heard about the raid."

"Then let's do it fast. Once Tinker sees something on the news, who knows what he'll do with some boy he has no market for."

"I'll have my undercover man talk with Shauna and see if she'll help. It appears she liked those girls she was stabling. She's out on bail and has offered to work with the social services people to get the girls situated. Apparently, Shauna came off the streets, just like these girls, and she cares for them. So, maybe she'll help us to save this boy. I'll call you to tell you how it goes down."

Liz had gone outside to make her calls, so she came back inside. The Lilliquists had finished making their calls when Liz returned. "Only those two boys who remembered this Hanson guy," said Mr. Lilliquist. What can we do next? Do you think that Terry has been abducted?"

"I'm hopeful the State Police in Flint may have a lead. The man running that Flint brothel operation had placed an order for a young boy. In fact, I heard him talking about needing a boy, while I was held captive. A man called the motel yesterday, leaving a message that he 'found that young male you needed' and he 'wanted to deliver soon'. He said his name was Tinker. The Flint Police are going to convince the female accomplice from the brothel to call Tinker and make the delivery. We're hoping this is your son, and we can recover him before he is harmed."

"Oh, my God, Miss Trent," Joan Lilliquist said. "We never thought we had to keep a constant eye on our teenagers, especially the boys, in a nice neighborhood like ours. Thank God you were here to hear our story. We would not have even thought of making any calls until tomorrow, and by then, Terry could have been in even more danger. Thank you so much."

"We don't have him home yet, and this possibly could be a different boy, but everything seems to be adding up to this being your son," Liz said. "Somehow, we need to convince parents to warn their children, both girls, and boys, that they need to tell their parents anytime a stranger asks them to do anything out of the ordinary. And the parents need to ask questions and meet the adults in their children's lives. These traffickers usually don't just grab children off the street, because it might create a scene. They use things that will attract a teenager, such as your son wanting to play baseball. Travel teams usually have parents traveling with the team, so that should have been a danger sign."

"I'm hearing what you said, Miss Trent, and I must admit that I was very guilty," Mr. Lilliquist said. "I was too busy this summer to attend any of Terry's baseball games. When he said he'd been chosen for a travel team, it never occurred to me to question it. It's my fault that Terry is in danger. I can only hope your quick actions will result in him being safe. Thank you so much."

"This is becoming more common than you can imagine, Mr. Lilliquist. I'm going to speak positively, hoping this boy is Terry. So, when Terry comes home, please spread the word about what happened. Warn other parents to be more vigilant."

Liz's phone rang and she saw it was the Flint Captain calling. "Yes, Captain. Any good news?"

"Yes. Shauna agreed to call Tinker. Turns out she hates the guy, and she never wanted Luke to have boys in her stable because she had to keep them separate. She convinced Tinker to make the delivery tonight. She told Tinker that Luke was in bed with a bad case of the flu. We'll take care of rescuing the boy and arresting Tinker, but in case it is your boy from

Cadillac, I need one of the parents here to identify their son. Be sure to bring the parent's ID and ID proof for their son. The delivery will be in about one hour from now, and it's about two hours from Cadillac to here. Can you have one of the parents come to the Flint Post?"

"Of course, Captain. Thank Shauna for doing the right thing. I know she was an accomplice in some criminal activity, but she seemed to like these young people. It's hard to understand some people. Tell Shauna that I said thank you for saving this boy."

"Understood, Officer Trent. I'll tell her. I'll also tell the prosecutor about her cooperation. One of the social services counselors has been pleased with Shauna's cooperation and suggested she apply for a job with the agency after she serves her time. A strange turn of events. In Shauna's statement, she said she wished she had the same help available to these kids. Shauna probably came from an abusive home, like some of these girls. I'm impressed that she is willing to help them, rather than worrying only about herself."

"She will certainly understand the problems these girls have. I wish her luck. We'll get on the road right away," Liz said.

Curt was still under doctor's orders not to drive until his surgery healed, and he also felt that Steve had driven too many hours already that day, so Curt asked Lois if she was alert enough to make the round-trip to Flint and return. Liz wanted to go, as well as Steve, and of course, Mr. Lilliquist, who was too emotional to drive. They piled into Mr. Lilliquist's large van and headed to Flint. Mr. Lilliquist wanted to know more about Liz and how she got into such an unusual line of police work. When Curt and Steve told him about the abduction which took place in Hammond, the eventual involvement of Liz Trent, and the sting operation in the Kentucky Gentlemen's Club, Mr. Lilliquist said, "I guess I've led a sheltered life. This hardly seems possible. How do you put up with this as a career?" he asked Liz.

"Well, it does wear you down, and I've reached the point where I may have had enough of this hands-on work. I've decided to go to Law School so I can prosecute these perps. I'm hoping to get the same satisfaction, without the tension, and occasional terror I feel, like this last week."

They arrived at the Flint State Police Post and Liz saw that Mr. Lilliquist was shaking. Although it certainly appeared that this was going to be his son, Terry, she knew that if it wasn't, the prospects for a safe return were greatly diminished.

The Trooper at the Post's front desk remembered Liz and Steve from the motel raid, and he greeted them warmly. He then asked, "Would this other gentleman be a Mr. Lilliquist? The young man in the back says his name is Terry Lilliquist. If you can show me some ID for you and your son, I'll let you go back to see him."

"Oh, thank God. I've been worried it wasn't Terry. Is he alright?"

"He was pretty scared, but it doesn't appear the guy had hurt him in any way. I don't think your son understood what he was headed for, so be prepared to answer those questions, Mr. Lilliquist. And, oh yes. Terry hadn't eaten all day and he was darn hungry. We've stuffed him with burgers, fries, and sodas, so he may have a terrible bellyache on the way home."

Liz, Lois, and Steve watched the very emotional reunion from an adjoining room. They could tell that Terry didn't fully understand his father's tears, probably never having seen his father cry before. They hoped Mr. Lilliquist might wait a few years to tell Terry of the full, terrible consequences of his abduction, but he would surely take a more active role in his children's lives after this experience.

Liz grabbed Steve's hand and laid her head against his shoulder with tears running down her face. From across the room, Lois saw them together and smiled. *'If they ended up together, who was going to be protecting who?'* She thought to herself. But does it really matter? They certainly seemed good together!

AUTHOR'S NOTE

If you read my Bio, you might wonder why I wrote this book, and also how I have any knowledge about Human Trafficking. During my career, I spent 7-1/2 years working for the Army Corps of Engineers, and we had to take the same training as active-duty Army soldiers. Each year, we went through Human Trafficking Awareness training, and the first time I thought, "This is silly. That's just a Third World problem."

Well, I was shocked to find out that Human Trafficking for "sexploitation" is worse in the United States than anywhere in the world. I started listening more closely, and the training was good. It gave many case studies showing how young teens, runaways mostly, are lured into "sex stables" when they are cold, hungry, and looking for an understanding person to listen to them. My story tried to show the different ways the young women are controlled, using violence, threats, and drugs, but also the "smart" ones who use kindness, which Liz called brainwashing.

If you are wondering if there will be another novel

on this subject, the answer is YES! I don't like those "series" of novels, which leave you hanging and you need to buy another book to hear the end of the story, so this book had an ending. But if you like Liz and Steve, they are in the second novel, coming out later this year. Liz is a lawyer, but still gets involved in trafficking, including very young children, imported from Asia. Yes, there are some very sick people in this world!